ANTON CHEKHOV
THE STEPPE

Translated from the Russian by
CONSTANCE GARNETT

ALAN SUTTON · Gloucester
HIPPOCRENE BOOKS, INC. · New York

First published 1919

Copyright © in this edition 1987
Alan Sutton Publishing Limited

This edition first published in Great Britain 1987
  Alan Sutton Publishing Limited
  30 Brunswick Road
  Gloucester GL1 1JJ

British Library Cataloguing in Publication Data

Chekhov, A.P.
  The Steppe.
  I. Title
  891.73'3 [F]   PG3456.S7

  ISBN 0-86299-361-X

This edition first published in the U.S.A. 1987
  Hippocrene Books, Inc.
  171 Madison Avenue
  New York, N.Y. 10016

  ISBN 0-87052-488-7

Cover picture: detail from A Corn Field
by Shishkin. Photograph: Novosti Press Agency

Typesetting and origination by
Alan Sutton Publishing Limited
Photoset Bembo 9/10.
Printed in Great Britain
by The Guernsey Press Company Limited,
Guernsey, Channel Islands.

BIOGRAPHICAL NOTE

Anton Pavlovich Chekhov was a Russian of remarkable talent. He was a medical doctor, with a great respect for science, and a writer with a mystical awareness, a fine appreciation of the dual nature of humanity and of the world, and a realisation of the horror and of the beauty of earthly existence. He conveyed his observations always with clear-sighted truthfulness, often with humour, and sometimes with poignant lyricism in the many stories and the few plays which he wrote during his short life. He was an individual who allied himself with no religion, nor with any political party; yet he lead a strictly ethical life, and was actively concerned with the social conditions he found around him.

His grandfather was born a serf, but had been resourceful enough to make sufficient money to buy his family's freedom. Chekhov's father, on the other hand, was more religious and artistic than practical, and made little success of providing for his wife and six children in the general store where the family lived in Taganrog, a small harbour town on the Sea of Azov in Southern Russia. Anton, born on 17 January 1860, was the third son, and he and his two elder brothers were, from an early age, called upon to work for long hours in the shop and chant for long hours in the church. The physical conditions of those early years were wretched, and it is not surprising that Anton and one of his brothers developed consumption in their twenties. Although home comforts were in short supply, education was not, and Anton attended the local state school until he was nineteen. During that time he had his first experience of the theatre, when touring companies visited Taganrog. The boys had to obtain permission from school for every performance they wished to attend, so the light-hearted Chekhov would often go in disguise, heavily made-up to avoid recognition by monitoring teachers. Before he left school, his father was forced to flee to Moscow for financial reasons; his two elder brothers were already there, and his mother and younger sister and brothers soon followed, leaving Anton to sell off their effects and provide for himself by giving private lessons while he finished his schooling.

At nineteen, however, Chekhov left Taganrog and went to Moscow, entering the medical faculty of the University and living in slum conditions with his family. One year later he started writing, to make money. He wrote short stories, often humorous, for journals and magazines in Moscow and St Petersberg. In 1880 he sold nine of them; by 1885 he was producing more than a hundred pieces of work a year. His first collection in book form was published in 1884, after he had completed his medical training. Two years later he was asked to write regularly for *Novoye Vremia*, the most influential Russian daily, and he received an important letter of encouragement from the novelist Grigorovich, finally convincing him of his talent as a writer, and making him take his writing more seriously than in the past. He continued with short stories, but also experimented in the field of drama, producing five one act sketches which he called 'vaudevilles', and two full-length plays: *Ivanov* and *The Wood Demon* (later to be re-written as *Uncle Vanya*).

Socially and financially Chekhov was now well-established and able to move with his mother, sister Maria, and younger brother into the house in Sadovaia-Kudrinskaia, where he lived until 1892, and which is now the Chekhov Museum. He had achieved a position among the cultural élite of Moscow. One of his life-long friendships which dated from those days was with the Romantic painter, Levitan, and another was with Suvorin, the editor of *Novoye Vremia*. He also had a close relationship with his sister, but, although he had friendships with women – he was both handsome and charming – he committed himself to none, feeling that in order to do justice to his talents, he must maintain emotional independence.

It was during those years that his consumption made itself unpleasantly evident. His elder brother, Nicholas, was worse affected, and died in 1889. This loss was one of the motivating forces which made Chekhov decide to visit the grim island of Sakhalin. He had started to prepare a thesis on the history of medicine, but then realised that he would prefer to study a topic more immediate and relevant. So, in spite of poor health, he made the terrific journey across Russia (before the railway was opened) to Sakhalin Island, just North of Japan, to study and make a detailed report on the Russian convict colony out there. Chekhov was profoundly moved by the human degradation he witnessed – an example of the horror of the world. He wrote factually and directly about his findings in *The Island of Sakhalin*, and fictionally and indirectly in various short stories, *Murder in Exile*, *Groussev*, *The Babas* and others. Drained by the shock of his experiences, he longed for culture, beauty and comfort when he returned home, finding these on his first visit to Europe in 1891.

He travelled in Europe on several occasions during the next ten years, but never came to England. He was in Paris at the time of the Dreyfus Affair, and admired and supported Emile Zola's defence of the Jew. On one occasion, he bought books in Nice for the public library in Taganrog.

Although Chekhov enjoyed his visits abroad, he prefered to work at home. For the benefit of his health, and to ensure the privacy which he needed in order to work, he left Moscow in 1892 and bought an estate outside the city at Melikhovo. He loved his new home and garden and found peace in the natural surroundings. He was now in his thirties, aware that he was not immortal, and frustrated by the apparent worthlessness of his life. He had been affected briefly by Tolstoy's grand philosophy, but realised that, for him, truth was not to be found in the thoughts of others, that there was no overall pattern, reason or order in the world. He admitted his feeling of ignorance: 'We shall not try to play the quack but will admit frankly that we cannot understand anything in this world. Only imbeciles and quacks understand and know everything,' he wrote to a friend. For Chekhov, as for the mystic, reality was to be found in the moment, in isolation. He thought that the only purpose of literature was to portray the truth as the writer perceived it: 'Man will only grow better when he has seen himself as he is'. But he longed to do something noble and significant with his life: 'To save his soul, the Muslim digs a well. It would be a good thing if each of us left behind him a school, a well or something else, so that one's life should not pass and be lost in eternity without leaving a trace of its passage on this earth', he wrote in his diary.

During the next six years Chekhov fulfilled this desire to benefit the common good. He maintained a demanding medical practice and funded and established three schools in the area, as well as supplying various libraries. He was awarded a 'hereditary nobility' by Nicholas II for his 'exemplary zeal and exertions directed towards the education of the people.' It was during these years that Chekhov wrote *The Muzhiks*, an important story about peasant life, *The Black Monk*, and *Ward 6*, which attacked some aspects of Tolstoy's philosophy. He also wrote *The Seagull*, which was produced in St Petersberg in 1896, and a disastrous failure.

When he was thirty-seven, Chekhov's health had deteriorated to such an extent that he was recommended to move south. So in 1898 he had a new house and a new garden to create, this time on the outskirts of Yalta, on the Crimea. Once again he became involved in welfare work, his major achievement being the establishment of the Chekhov Sanitorium, for which he personally requested subscriptions from affluent Russians. During those last years of his life, he became friends with the young novelists Bunin, Kuprin and Gorki. It was in support of the latter, whom he saw as a destroyer of evil, that Chekhov resigned from the Moscow Academy of Belles Lettres. Another important connection was that with the newly-formed Moscow Arts Theatre, under the direction of Nemirovich-Danchenko and Stanislavski. The company successfully performed *The Seagull* in 1898, followed soon after by *Uncle Vanya* (1899). Chekhov met and fell in love with one of the leading actresses, Olga Knipper, and it was for her that he wrote *The Three Sisters* (1901). His final play, *The Cherry Orchard*, was first produced by the company a few months before his death in January, 1904.

Stanislavski, in his autobiography, gives a few personal glimpses of Chekhov. Of his genius he says: 'Chekhov, like no one else, was able to create inward and outward artistic truth. This is why he was able to say the truth about men.' He recalls that Chekhov had very little to say about the manner of the production of his plays, but that he was 'very proud of his medical calling, much more than of his talents as a writer.' He remembers Chekhov's humour: 'it was impossible not to laugh in Chekhov's presence', and he relates the practical joke Chekhov played on the theatre company, when he invited them all to supper at a friend's house while he went off and quietly married Olga Knipper, thus avoiding all ceremony and the hated embarrassment of being a centre of attention.

In 1901 Chekhov married. He and Olga lived apart much of the time, as she continued with her career and he was unable to spend long in Moscow, but she went with him on his last visit to Europe, and was with him when he died on a night early in July 1904, at the Black Forest sanitorium of Badenweiler. His body was later interred in the cemetery of the New Maiden Convent in Moscow.

SHEILA MICHELL

CHAPTER I

Early one morning in July a shabby covered chaise, one of those antediluvian chaises without springs in which no one travels in Russia nowadays, except merchants' clerks, dealers and the less well-to-do among priests, drove out of N., the principal town of the the province of Z., and rumbled noisily along the posting-track. It rattled and creaked at every movement; the pail, hanging on behind, chimed in gruffly, and from these sounds alone and from the wretched rags of leather hanging loose about its peeling body one could judge of its decrepit age and readiness to drop to pieces.

Two of the inhabitants of N. were sitting in the chaise; they were a merchant of N. called Ivan Ivanitch Kuzmitchov, a man with a shaven face, wearing glasses and a straw hat, more like a government clerk than a merchant, and Father Christopher Sireysky, the priest of the Church of St. Nikolay at N., a little old man with long hair, in a grey canvas cassock, a wide-brimmed top-hat and a coloured embroidered girdle. The former was absorbed in thought, and kept tossing his head to shake off drowsiness; in his countenance an habitual business-like reserve was struggling with the genial expression of a man who has just said good-bye to his relatives and has had a good drink at parting. The latter gazed with moist eyes wonderingly at God's world, and his smile was so broad that it seemed to embrace even the brim of his hat; his face was red and looked frozen. Both of them, Father Christopher as well as Kuzmitchov, were going to sell wool. At parting with their families they had just eaten heartily of pastry puffs and cream, and although it was so early in the morning had had a glass or two. . . . Both were in the best of humours.

Apart from the two persons described above and the coachman Deniska, who lashed the pair of frisky bay horses, there was another figure in the chaise – a boy of nine with a sunburnt face, wet with tears. This was Yegorushka, Kuzmit-

chov's nephew. With the sanction of his uncle and the blessing
of Father Christopher, he was now on his way to go to school.
His mother, Olga Ivanovna, the widow of a collegiate
secretary, and Kuzmitchov's sister, who was fond of educated
people and refined society, had entreated her brother to take
Yegorushka with him when he went to sell wool and to put
him to school; and now the boy was sitting on the box beside
the coachman Deniska, holding on to his elbow to keep from
falling off, and dancing up and down like a kettle on the hob,
with no notion where he was going or what he was going for.
The rapid motion through the air blew out his red shirt like a
balloon on his back and made his new hat with a peacock's
feather in it, like a coachman's, keep slipping on to the back of
his head. He felt himself an intensely unfortunate person, and
had an inclination to cry.

When the chaise drove past the prison, Yegorushka glanced
at the sentinels pacing slowly by the high white walls, at the
little barred windows, at the cross shining on the roof, and
remembered how the week before, on the day of the Holy
Mother of Kazan, he had been with his mother to the prison
church for the Dedication Feast, and how before that, at
Easter, he had gone to the prison with Deniska and Ludmila
the cook, and had taken the prisoners Easter bread, eggs, cakes
and roast beef. The prisoners had thanked them and made the
sign of the cross, and one of them had given Yegorushka a
pewter buckle of his own making.

The boy gazed at the familiar places, while the hateful chaise
flew by and left them all behind. After the prison he caught
glimpses of black grimy foundries, followed by the snug
green cemetery surrounded by a wall of cobblestones; white
crosses and tombstones, nestling among green cherry-trees
and looking in the distance like patches of white, peeped out
gaily from behind the wall. Yegorushka remembered that
when the cherries were in blossom those white patches melted
with the flowers into a sea of white; and that when the cherries
were ripe the white tombstones and crosses were dotted with
splashes of red like bloodstains. Under the cherry-trees in the
cemetery Yegorushka's father and granny, Zinaida
Danilovna, lay sleeping day and night. When Granny had died
she had been put in a long narrow coffin and two pennies had

been put upon her eyes, which would not keep shut. Up to the time of her death she had been brisk, and used to bring soft rolls covered with poppy seeds from the market. Now she did nothing but sleep and sleep. . . .

Beyond the cemetery came the smoking brickyards. From under the long roofs of reeds that looked as though pressed flat to the ground, a thick black smoke rose in great clouds and floated lazily upwards. The sky was murky above the brickyards and the cemetery, and great shadows from the clouds of smoke crept over the fields and across the roads. Men and horses covered with red dust were moving about in the smoke near the roofs. . . .

The town ended with the brickyards and the open country began. Yegorushka looked at the town for the last time, pressed his face against Deniska's elbow, and wept bitterly. . . .

'Come, not done howling yet, cry-baby!' cried Kuzmitchov. 'You are blubbering again, little milksop! If you don't want to go, stay behind; no one is taking you by force!'

'Never mind, never mind, Yegor boy, never mind,' Father Christopher muttered rapidly – 'never mind, my boy. . . . Call upon God. . . . You are not going for your harm, but for your good. Learning is light, as the saying is, and ignorance is darkness. . . . That is so, truly.'

'Do you want to go back?' asked Kuzmitchov.

'Yes, . . . yes, . . .' answered Yegorushka, sobbing.

'Well, you'd better go back then. Anyway, you are going for nothing; it's a day's journey for a spoonful of porridge.'

'Never mind, never mind, my boy,' Father Christopher went on, 'Call upon God. . . . Lomonosov set off with the fishermen in the same way, and he became a man famous all over Europe. Learning in conjunction with faith brings forth fruit pleasing to God. What are the words of the prayer? For the glory of our Maker, for the comfort of our parents, for the benefit of our Church and our country. . . . Yes, indeed!'

'The benefit is not the same in all cases,' said Kuzmitchov, lighting a cheap cigar; 'some will study twenty years and get no sense from it.'

'That does happen.'

'Learning is a benefit to some, but others only muddle their brains. My sister is a woman who does not understand; she is set upon refinement, and wants to turn Yegorka into a learned man, and she does not understand that with my business I could settle Yegorka happily for the rest of his life. I tell you this, that if everyone were to go in for being learned and refined there would be no one to sow the corn and do the trading; they would all die of hunger.'

'And if all go in for trading and sowing corn there will be no one to acquire learning.'

And considering that each of them had said something weighty and convincing, Kuzmitchov and Father Christopher both looked serious and cleared their throats simultaneously.

Deniska, who had been listening to their conversation without understanding a word of it, shook his head and, rising in his seat, lashed at both the bays. A silence followed.

Meanwhile a wide boundless plain encircled by a chain of low hills lay stretched before the traveller's eyes. Huddling together and peeping out from behind one another, these hills melted together into rising ground, which stretched right to the very horizon and disappeared into the lilac distance; one drives on and on and cannot discern where it begins or where it ends. . . The sun had already peeped out from beyond the town behind them and quietly, without fuss, set to its accustomed task. At first in the distance before them a broad, bright, yellow streak of light crept over the ground where the earth met the sky, near the little barrows and the windmills, which in the distance looked like tiny men waving their arms. A minute later a similar streak gleamed a little nearer, crept to the right and embraced the hills. Something warm touched Yegorushka's spine; the streak of light, stealing up from behind, darted between the chaise and the horses, moved to meet the other streak, and soon the whole wide steppe flung off the twilight of early morning, and was smiling and sparkling with dew.

The cut rye, the coarse steppe grass, the milkwort, the wild hemp, all withered from the sultry heat, turned brown and half dead, now washed by the dew and caressed by the sun, revived, to fade again. Arctic petrels flew across the road with joyful cries; marmots called to one another in the grass. Somewhere, far away to the left, lapwings uttered their plaintive notes. A covey of partridges, scared by the chaise, fluttered up and with their soft 'trrrr!' flew off to the hills. In the grass crickets, locusts and grasshoppers kept up their churring, monotonous music.

But a little time passed, the dew evaporated, the air grew stagnant, and the disillusioned steppe began to wear its jaded July aspect. The grass drooped, everything living was hushed. The sun-baked hills, brownish-green and lilac in the distance, with their quiet shadowy tones, the plain with the misty distance and, arched above them, the sky, which seems terribly deep and transparent in the steppes, where there are no woods or high hills, seemed now endless, petrified with dreariness. . . .

How stifling and oppressive it was! The chaise raced along, while Yegorushka saw always the same – the sky, the plain, the low hills. . . . The music in the grass was hushed, the petrels had flown away, the partridges were out of sight, rooks hovered idly over the withered grass; they were all alike and made the steppe even more monotonous.

A hawk flew just above the ground, with an even sweep of its wings, suddenly halted in the air as though pondering on the dreariness of life, then fluttered its wings and flew like an arrow over the steppe, and there was no telling why it flew off and what it wanted. In the distance a windmill waved its sails. . . .

Now and then a glimpse of a white potsherd or a heap of stones broke the monotony; a grey stone stood out for an instant or a parched willow with a blue crow on its top branch; a marmot would run across the road and – again there flitted before the eyes only the high grass, the low hills, the rooks. . . .

But at last, thank God, a waggon loaded with sheaves came to meet them; a peasant wench was lying on the very top. Sleepy, exhausted by the heat, she lifted her head and looked at the travellers. Deniska gaped, looking at her; the horses stretched out their noses towards the sheaves; the chaise, squeaking, kissed the waggon, and the pointed ears passed over Father Christopher's hat like a brush.

'You are driving over folks, fatty!' cried Deniska. 'What a swollen lump of a face, as though a bumble-bee had stung it!'

The girl smiled drowsily, and moving her lips lay down again; then a solitary poplar came into sight on the low hill.

Someone had planted it, and God only knows why it was there. It was hard to tear the eyes away from its graceful figure and green drapery. Was that lovely creature happy? Sultry heat in summer, in winter frost and snowstorms, terrible nights in autumn when nothing is to be seen but darkness and nothing is to be heard but the senseless angry howling wind, and, worst of all, alone, alone for the whole of life. . . . Beyond the poplar stretches of wheat extended like a bright yellow carpet from the road to the top of the hills. On the hills the corn was already cut and laid up in sheaves, while at the bottom they were still cutting. . . . Six mowers were standing in a row swinging their scythes, and the scythes gleamed gaily and uttered in unison together 'Vzhee, vzhee!' From the movements of the peasant women binding the sheaves, from the faces of the mowers, from the glitter of the scythes, it could be seen that the sultry heat was baking and stifling. A black dog with its tongue hanging out ran from the mowers to meet the chaise, probably with the intention of barking, but stopped halfway and stared indifferently at Deniska, who shook his whip at him; it was too hot to bark! One peasant woman got up and, putting both hands to her aching back, followed Yegorushka's red shirt with her eyes. Whether it was that the colour pleased her or that it reminded her of her children, she stood a long time motionless staring after him. . . .

But now the wheat, too, had flashed by; again the parched plain, the sunburnt hills, the sultry sky stretched before them; again a hawk hovered over the earth. In the distance, as before, a windmill whirled its sails, and still it looked like a little man waving his arms. It was wearisome to watch, and it seemed as though one would never reach it, as though it were running away from the chaise.

Father Christopher and Kuzmitchov were silent. Deniska lashed the horses and kept shouting to them, while Yegorushka had left off crying, and gazed about him listlessly. The heat and the tedium of the steppes overpowered him. He felt as though he had been travelling and jolting up and down for a very long time, that the sun had been baking his back a long time. Before they had gone eight miles he began to feel, 'It must be time to rest'. The geniality gradually faded out of his uncle's face, and nothing else was left but the air of business reserve; and to a gaunt shaven face, especially when it is adorned with spectacles and the nose and temples are covered with dust, this reserve gives a relentless, inquisitorial appearance. Father Christopher never left off gazing with wonder at God's world, and smiling. Without speaking, he brooded over something pleasant and nice, and a kindly, genial smile remained imprinted on his face. It seemed as though some nice and pleasant thought were imprinted on his brain by the heat. . . .

'Well, Deniska, shall we overtake the waggons today?' asked Kuzmitchov.

Deniska looked at the sky, rose in his seat, lashed at his horses and then answered:

'By nightfall, please God, we shall overtake them.'

There was a sound of dogs barking. Half a dozen steppe sheep-dogs, suddenly leaping out as though from ambush, with ferocious howling barks, flew to meet the chaise. All of them, extraordinarily furious, surrounded the chaise, with their shaggy spider-like muzzles and their eyes red with anger, and jostling against one another in their anger, raised a hoarse howl. They were filled with passionate hatred of the horses, of the chaise, and of the human beings, and seemed ready to tear them to pieces. Deniska, who was fond of teasing and beating, was delighted at the chance of it, and with a malignant expression bent over and lashed at the sheep-dogs with his whip. The brutes growled more than ever, the horses flew on; and Yegorushka, who had difficulty in keeping his seat on the box, realized, looking at the dogs' eyes and teeth, that if he fell down they would instantly tear him to bits; but he felt no fear and looked at them as malignantly as Deniska, and regretted that he had no whip in his hand.

The chaise came upon a flock of sheep.

'Stop!' cried Kuzmitchov. 'Pull up! Woa!'

Deniska threw his whole body backwards and pulled up the horses.

'Come here!' Kuzmitchov shouted to the shepherd. 'Call off the dogs, curse them!'

The old shepherd, tattered and barefoot, wearing a fur cap, with a dirty sack round his loins and a long crook in his hand –

a regular figure from the Old Testament – called off the dogs, and taking off his cap, went up to the chaise. Another similar Old Testament figure was standing motionless at the other end of the flock, staring without interest at the travellers.

'Whose sheep are these?' asked Kuzmitchov.

'Varlamov's,' the old man answered in a loud voice.

'Varlamov's,' repeated the shepherd standing at the other end of the flock.

'Did Varlamov come this way yesterday or not?'

'He did not; his clerk came. . .'

'Drive on!'

The chaise rolled on and the shepherds, with their angry dogs, were left behind. Yegorushka gazed listlessly at the lilac distance in front, and it began to seem as though the windmill, waving its sails, was getting nearer. It became bigger and bigger, grew quite large, and now he could distinguish clearly its two sails. One sail was old and patched, the other had only lately been made of new wood and glistened in the sun. The chaise drove straight on, while the windmill, for some reason, began retreating to the left. They drove on and on, and the windmill kept moving away to the left, and still did not disappear.

'A fine windmill Boltva has put up for his son,' observed Deniska.

'And how is it we don't see his farm?'

'It is that way, beyond the creek.'

Boltva's farm, too, soon came into sight, but yet the windmill did not retreat, did not drop behind; it still watched Yegorushka with its shining sail and waved. What a sorcerer!

CHAPTER II

Towards midday the chaise turned off the road to the right; it went on a little way at walking pace and then stopped. Yegorushka heard a soft, very caressing gurgle, and felt a different air breathe on his face with a cool velvety touch. Through a little pipe of hemlock stuck there by some unknown benefactor, water was running in a thin trickle from a low hill, put together by nature of huge monstrous stones. It fell to the ground, and limpid, sparkling gaily in the sun, and softly murmuring as though fancying itself a great tempestuous torrent, flowed swiftly away to the left. Not far from its source the little stream spread itself out into a pool; the burning sunbeams and the parched soil greedily drank it up and sucked away its strength; but a little further on it must have mingled with another rivulet, for a hundred paces away thick reeds showed green and luxuriant along its course, and three snipe flew up from them with a loud cry as the chaise drove by.

The travellers got out to rest by the stream and feed the horses. Kuzmitchov, Father Christopher and Yegorushka sat down on a mat in the narrow strip of shade cast by the chaise and the unharnessed horses. The nice pleasant thought that the heat had imprinted in Father Christopher's brain craved expression after he had had a drink of water and eaten a hard-boiled egg. He bent a friendly look upon Yegorushka, munched, and began:

'I studied too, my boy; from the earliest age God instilled into me good sense and understanding, so that while I was just such a lad as you I was beyond others, a comfort to my parents and preceptors by my good sense. Before I was fifteen I could speak and make verses in Latin, just as in Russian. I was the crosier-bearer to his Holiness Bishop Christopher. After mass one day, as I remember it was the patron saint's day of His Majesty Tsar Alexandr Pavlovitch of blessed memory, he

9

unrobed at the altar, looked kindly at me and asked, "Puer bone, quam appelaris?" And I answered, "Christopherus sum," and he said, "Ergo connominati sumus" – that is, that we were namesakes. . . Then he asked in Latin, "Whose son are you?" To which I answered, also in Latin, "that I was the son of deacon Sireysky of the village of Lebedinskoe". Seeing my readiness and the clearness of my answers, his Holiness blessed me and said, "Write to your father that I will not forget him, and that I will keep you in view." The holy priests and fathers who were standing round the altar, hearing our discussion in Latin, were not a little surprised, and everyone expressed his pleasure in praise of me. Before I had moustaches, my boy, I could read Latin, Greek, and French; I knew philosophy, mathematics, secular history, and all the sciences. The Lord gave me a marvellous memory. Sometimes, if I read a thing once or twice, I knew it by heart. My preceptors and patrons were amazed, and so they expected I should make a learned man, a luminary of the Church. I did think of going to Kiev to continue my studies, but my parents did not approve. "You'll be studying all your life," said my father; "when shall we see you finished?" Hearing such words, I gave up study and took a post. . . Of course, I did not become a learned man, but then I did not disobey my parents; I was a comfort to them in their old age and gave them a creditable funeral. Obedience is more than fasting and prayer.'

'I suppose you have forgotten all your learning?' observed Kuzmitchov.

'I should think so! Thank God, I have reached my eightieth year! Something of philosophy and rhetoric I do remember, but languages and mathematics I have quite forgotten.'

Father Christopher screwed up his eyes, thought a minute and said in an undertone:

'What is a substance? A creature is a self-existing object, not requiring anything else for its completion.'

He shook his head and laughed with feeling.

'Spiritual nourishment!' he said. 'Of a truth matter nourishes the flesh and spiritual nourishment the soul!'

'Learning is all very well,' sighed Kuzmitchov, 'but if we don't overtake Varlamov, learning won't do much for us.'

'A man isn't a needle – we shall find him. He must be going his rounds in these parts.'

Among the sedge were flying the three snipe they had seen before, and in their plaintive cries there was a note of alarm and vexation at having been driven away from the stream. The horses were steadily munching and snorting. Deniska walked about by them and, trying to appear indifferent to the cucumbers, pies, and eggs that the gentry were eating, he concentrated himself on the gadflies and horseflies that were fastening upon the horses' backs and bellies; he squashed his victims apathetically, emitting a peculiar, fiendishly triumphant, guttural sound, and when he missed them cleared his throat with an air of vexation and looked after every lucky one that escaped death.

'Deniska, where are you? Come and eat,' said Kuzmitchov, heaving a deep sigh, a sign that he had had enough.

Deniska diffidently approached the mat and picked out five thick and yellow cucumbers (he did not venture to take the smaller and fresher ones), took two hard-boiled eggs that looked dark and were cracked, then irresolutely, as though afraid he might get a blow on his outstretched hand, touched a pie with his finger.

'Take them, take them,' Kuzmitchov urged him on.

Deniska took the pies resolutely, and, moving some distance away, sat down on the grass with his back to the chaise. At once there was such a sound of loud munching that even the horses turned round to look suspiciously at Deniska.

After his meal Kuzmitchov took a sack containing something out of the chaise and said to Yegorushka:

'I am going to sleep, and you mind that no one takes the sack from under my head.'

Father Christopher took off his cassock, his girdle, and his full coat, and Yegorushka, looking at him, was dumb with astonishment. He had never imagined that priests wore trousers, and Father Christopher had on real canvas trousers thrust high into his boots, and a short striped jacket. Looking at him, Yegorushka thought that in this costume, so unsuitable to his dignified position, he looked with his long hair and beard very much like Robinson Crusoe. After taking off their outer garments Kuzmitchov and Father Christopher lay down in the

shade under the chaise, facing one another, and closed their
eyes. Deniska, who had finished munching, stretched himself
out on his back and also closed his eyes.

'You look out that no one takes away the horses!' he said to
Yegorushka, and at once fell asleep.

Stillness reigned. There was no sound except the munching
and snorting of the horses and the snoring of the sleepers;
somewhere far away a lapwing wailed, and from time to time
there sounded the shrill cries of the three snipe who had flown
up to see whether their uninvited visitors had gone away; the
rivulet babbled, lisping softly, but all these sounds did not
break the stillness, did not stir the stagnation, but, on the
contrary, lulled all nature to slumber.

Yegorushka, gasping with the heat, which was particularly
oppressive after a meal, ran to the sedge and from there
surveyed the country. He saw exactly the same as he had in the
morning: the plain, the low hills, the sky, the lilac distance;
only the hills stood nearer; and he could not see the windmill,
which had been left far behind. From behind the rocky hill
from which the stream flowed rose another, smoother and
broader; a little hamlet of five or six homesteads clung to it.
No people, no trees, no shade were to be seen about the huts;
it looked as though the hamlet had expired in the burnin air
and was dried up. To while away the time Yegorushka caught
a grasshopper in the grass, held it in his closed hand to his ear,
and spent a long time listening to the creature playing on its
instrument. When he was weary of its music he ran after a
flock of yellow butterflies who were flying toward the sedge
on the watercourse, and found himself again beside the chaise,
without noticing how he came there. His uncle and Father
Christopher were sound asleep; their sleep would be sure to
last two or three hours till the horses had rested. . . . How
was he to get through that long time, and where was he to get
away from the heat? A hard problem. . . . Mechanically
Yegorushka put his lips to the trickle that ran from the
waterpipe; there was a chilliness in his mouth and there was
the smell of hemlock. He drank at first eagerly, the went on
with effort till the sharp cold had run from his mouth all over
his body and the water was spilt on his shirt. Then he went up
to the chaise and began looking at the sleeping figures. His

uncle's face wore, as before, an expression of businesslike reserve. Fanatically devoted to his work, Kuzmitchov always, even in his sleep and at church when they were singing, 'Like the cherubim', thought about his business and could not forget it for a moment; and now he was probably dreaming about bales of wool, waggons, prices, Varlamov. . . . Father Christopher, now, a soft, frivolous and absurd person, had never in all his life been conscious of anything which could, like a boa-constrictor, coil about his soul and hold it tight. In all the numerous enterprises he had undertaken in his day what attracted him was not so much the business itself, but the bustle and the contact with other people involved in every undertaking. Thus, in the present expedition, he was not so much interested in wool, in Varlamov, and in prices, as in the long journey, the conversations on the way, the sleeping under a chaise, and the meals at odd times. . . And now, judging from his face, he must have been dreaming of Bishop Christopher, of the Latin discussion, of his wife, of puffs and cream and all sorts of things that Kuzmitchov could not possible dream of.

While Yegorushka was watching their sleeping faces he suddenly heard a soft singing; somewhere at a distance a woman was singing, and it was difficult to tell where and in what direction. The song was subdued, dreary and melancholy, like a dirge, and hardly audible, and seemed to come first from the right, then from the left, then from above, and then from underground, as though an unseen spirit were hovering over the steppe and singing. Yegorushka looked about him, and could not make out where the strange song came from. Then as he listened he began to fancy that the grass was singing; in its song, withered and half-dead, it was without words, but plaintively and passionately, urging that it was not to blame, that the sun was burning it for no fault of its own; it urged that it ardently longed to live, that it was young and might have been beautiful but for the heat and the drought; it was guiltless, but yet it prayed forgiveness and protested that it was in anguish, sad and sorry for itself. . . .

Yegorushka listened for a little, and it began to seem as though this dreary, mournful song made the air hotter, more suffocating and more stagnant. . . . To drown the singing he ran to the sedge, humming to himself and trying to make a noise with his feet. From there he looked about in all directions and found out who was singing. Near the furthest hut in the hamlet stood a peasant woman in a short petticoat, with long thin legs like a heron. She was sowing something. A white dust floated languidly from her sieve down the hillock. Now it was evident that she was singing. A couple of yards from her a little bare-headed boy in nothing but a smock was standing motionless. As though fascinated by the song, he stood stock-still, staring away into the distance, probably at Yegorushka's crimson shirt.

The song ceased. Yegorushka sauntered back to the chaise, and to while away the time went again to the trickle of water.

And again there was the sound of the dreary song. It was the same long-legged peasant woman in the hamlet over the hill. Yegorushka's boredom came back again. He left the pipe and looked upwards. What he saw was so unexpected that he was a little frightened. Just above his head on one of the big clumsy stones stood a chubby little boy, wearing nothing but a shirt, with a prominent stomach and thin legs, the same boy who had been standing before by the peasant woman. He was gazing with open mouth and unblinking eyes at Yegorushka's crimson shirt and at the chaise, with a look of blank astonishment and even fear, as though he saw before him creatures of another world. The red colour of the shirt charmed and allured him. But the chaise and the men sleeping under it excited his curiosity; perhaps he had not noticed how the agreeable red colour and curiosity had attracted him down from the hamlet, and now probably he was surprised at his own boldness. For a long while Yegorushka stared at him, and he at Yegorushka. Both were silent and conscious of some awkwardness. After a long silence Yegorushka asked:

'What's your name?'

The stranger's cheeks puffed out more than ever; he pressed his back against the rock, opened his eyes wide, moved his lips, and answered in a husky bass: 'Tit!'

The boys said not another word to each other; after a brief silence, still keeping his eyes fixed on Yegorushka, the mysterious Tit kicked up one leg, felt with his heel for a niche and clambered up the rock; from that point he ascended to the next rock, staggering backwards and looking intently at Yegorushka, as though afraid he might hit him from behind, and so made his way upwards till he disappeared altogether behind the crest of the hill.

After watching him out of sight, Yegorushka put his arms round his knees and leaned his head on them. . . . The burning sun scorched the back of his head, his neck, and his spine. The melancholy song died away, then floated again on the stagnant stifling air. The rivulet gurgled monotonously, the horses munched, and time dragged on endlessly, as though it, too, were stagnant and had come to a standstill. It seemed as though a hundred years had passed since the morning. Could it be that God's world, the chaise and the horses would come to a standstill in that air, and, like the hills, turn to stone and remain forever in one spot? Yegorushka raised his head and with smarting eyes looked before him; the lilac distance, which till then had been motionless, began heaving, and with the sky floated away into the distance. . . . It drew after it the brown grass, the sedge, and with extraordinary swiftness Yegorushka floated after the flying distance. Some force noiselessly drew him onwards, and the heat and the wearisome song flew after in pursuit. Yegorushka bent his head and shut his eyes. . . .

Deniska was the first to wake up. Something must have bitten him, for he jumped up, quickly scratched his shoulder and said:

'Plague take you, cursed idolater!'

Then he went to the brook, had a drink and slowly washed. His splashing and puffing roused Yegorushka from his lethargy. The boy looked at his wet face with drops of water and big freckles which made it look like marble, and asked:

'Shall we soon be going?'

Deniska looked at the height of the sun and answered:

'I expect so.'

He dried himself with the tail of his shirt and, making a very serious face, hopped on one leg.

'I say, which of us will get to the sedge first?' he said.

Yegorushka was exhausted by the heat and drowsiness, but raced off after him all the same. Deniska was in his twentieth year, was a coachman and going to be married, but he had not left off being a boy. He was very fond of flying kites, chasing pigeons, playing knuckle-bones, running races, and always took part in children's games and disputes. No sooner had his master turned his back or gone to sleep than Deniska would begin doing something such as hopping on one leg or throwing stones. It was hard for any grown-up person, seeing the genuine enthusiasm with which he frolicked about in the society of children, to resist saying, 'What a baby!' Children, on the other hand, saw nothing strange in the invasion of their domain by the big coachman. 'Let him play,' they thought, 'as long as he doesn't fight!' In the same way little dogs see nothing strange in it when a simple-hearted big dog joins their company uninvited and begins playing with them.

Deniska outstripped Yegorushka, and was evidently very much pleased at having done so. He winked at him, and to show that he could hop on one leg any distance, suggested to Yegorushka that he should hop with him along the road and from there, without resting, back to the chaise. Yegorushka declined this suggestion, for he was very much out of breath and exhausted.

All at once Deniska looked very grave, as he did not look even when Kuzmitchov gave him a scolding or threatened him with a stick; listening intently, he dropped quietly on one knee and an expression of sternness and alarm came into his face, such as one sees in people who hear heretical talk. He fixed his eyes on one spot, raised his hand curved into a hollow, and suddenly fell on his stomach on the ground and slapped the hollow of his hand down upon the grass.

'Caught!' he wheezed triumphantly, and, getting up, lifted a big grasshopper to Yegorushka's eyes.

The two boys stroked the grasshopper's broad green back with their fingers and touched his antennæ, supposing that this would please the creature. Then Deniska caught a fat fly that had been sucking blood and offered it to the grasshopper. The latter moved his huge jaws, that were like the visor of a helmet, with the utmost unconcern, as though he had been long acquainted with Deniska, and bit off the fly's stomach. They let him go. With a flash of the pink lining of his wings, he flew down into the grass and at once began his churring notes again. They let the fly go, too. It preened its wings, and without its stomach flew off to the horses.

A loud sigh was heard from under the chaise. It was Kuzmitchov waking up. He quickly raised his head, looked uneasily into the distance, and from that look, which passed by Yegorushka and Deniska without sympathy or interest, it could be seen that his thought on awaking was of the wool and of Varlamov.

'Father Christopher, get up; it is time to start,' he said anxiously. 'Wake up; we've slept too long as it is! Deniska, put the horses in.'

Father Christopher woke up with the same smile with which he had fallen asleep; his face looked creased and wrinkled from sleep, and seemed only half the size. After washing and dressing, he proceeded without haste to take out of his pocket a little greasy psalter; and standing with his face towards the east, began in a whisper repeating the psalms of the day and crossing himself.

'Father Christopher,' said Kuzmitchov reproachfully, 'it's time to start; the horses are ready, and here are you, . . .upon my word.'

'In a minute, in a minute,' muttered Father·Christopher. 'I must read the psalms. . . . I haven't read them to-day.'

'The psalms can wait.'

'Ivan Ivanitch, that is my rule every day. . . . I can't. . .'

'God will overlook it.'

For a full quarter of an hour Father Christopher stood facing the east and moving his lips, while Kuzmitchov looked at him almost with hatred and impatiently shrugged his shoulders. He was particularly irritated when, after every 'Hallelujah,' Father Christopher drew a long breath, rapidly crossed himself and repeated three times, intentionally raising his voice so that the others might cross themselves, 'Hallelujah, hallelujah, hallelujah! Glory be to Thee, O Lord!' At last he smiled, looked upwards at the sky, and, putting the psalter in his pocket, said *'Finis!'*

A minute later the chaise had started on the road. As though it were going backwards and not forwards, the travellers saw the same scene as they had before midday.

The low hills were still plunged in the lilac distance, and no end could be seen to them. There were glimpses of high grass and heaps of stones; strips of stubble land passed by them and still the same rooks, the same hawk, moving its wings with slow dignity, moved over the steppe. The air was more sultry than ever; from the sultry heat and the stillness submissive nature was spellbound into silence. . . . No wind, no fresh cheering sound, no cloud.

But at last, when the sun was beginning to sink into the west, the steppe, the hills and the air could bear the oppression no longer, and, driven out of all patience, exhausted, tried to fling off the yoke. A fleecy ashen-grey cloud unexpectedly appeared behind the hills. It exchanged glances with the steppe, as though to say, 'Here I am,' and frowned. Suddenly something burst in the stagnant air; there was a violent squall of wind which whirled round and round, roaring and whistling over the steppe. At once a murmur rose from the grass and last year's dry herbage, the dust curled in spiral eddies over the road, raced over the steppe, and carrying with it straws, dragon flies and feathers, rose up in a whirling black column towards the sky and darkened the sun. Prickly uprooted plants ran stumbling and leaping in all directions over the steppe, and one of them got caught in the whirlwind, turned round and round like a bird, flew towards the sky, and turning into a little black speck, vanished from sight. After it flew another, and then a third, and Yegorushka saw two of them meet in the blue height and clutch at one another as though they were wrestling.

A bustard flew up by the very road. Fluttering his wings and his tail, he looked, bathed in the sunshine, like an angler's glittering tin fish or a waterfly flashing so swiftly over the water that its wings cannot be told from its antennæ, which seem to be growing before, behind and on all sides. . . . Quivering in the air like an insect with a shimmer of bright colours, the bustard flew high up in a straight line, then, probably frightened by a cloud of dust, swerved to one side, and for a long time the gleam of his wings could be seen. . . .

Then a corncrake flew up from the grass, alarmed by the hurricane and not knowing what was the matter. It flew with the wind and not against it, like all the other birds, so that all its feathers were ruffled up and it was puffed out to the size of a hen and looked very angry and impressive. Only the rooks who had grown old on the steppe and were accustomed to its vagaries hovered calmly over the grass, or taking no notice of anything, went on unconcernedly pecking with their stout beaks at the hard earth.

There was a dull roll of thunder beyond the hills; there came a whiff of fresh air. Deniska gave a cheerful whistle and lashed his horses. Father Christopher and Kuzmitchov held their hats and looked intently towards the hills. . . . How pleasant a shower of rain would have been!

One effort, one struggle more, and it seemed the steppe would have got the upper hand. But the unseen oppressive force gradually riveted its fetters on the wind and the air, laid the dust, and the stillness came back again as though nothing had happened, the cloud hid, the sun-baked hills frowned submissively, the air grew calm, and only somewhere the troubled lapwings wailed and lamented their destiny. . . .

Soon after that the evening came on.

CHAPTER III

In the dusk of evening a big house of one storey, with a rusty iron roof and with dark windows, came into sight. This house was called a posting-inn, though it had nothing like a stableyard, and it stood in the middle of the steppe, with no kind of enclosure round it. A little to one side of it a wretched little cherry orchard shut in by a hurdle fence made a dark patch, and under the windows stood sleepy sunflowers drooping their heavy heads. From the orchard came the clatter of a little toy windmill, set there to frighten away hares by the rattle. Nothing more could be seen near the house, and nothing could be heard but the steppe. The chaise had scarcely stopped at the porch with an awning over it, when from the house there came the sound of cheerful voices, one a man's, another a woman's; there was the creak of a swing-door, and in a flash a tall gaunt figure, swinging its arms and fluttering its coat, was standing by the chaise. This was the inn-keeper, Moisey Moisevitch, a man no longer young, with a very pale face and a handsome beard as black as charcoal. He was wearing a threadbare black coat, which hung flapping on his narrow shoulders as though on a hatstand, and fluttered its skirts like wings every time Moisey Moisevitch flung up his hands in delight or horror. Besides his coat the innkeeper was wearing full white trousers, not stuck into his boots, and a velvet waistcoat with brown flowers on it that looked like gigantic bugs.

Moisey Moisevitch was at first dumb with excess of feeling on recognising the travellers, then he clasped his hands and uttered a moan. His coat swung its skirts, his back bent into a bow, and his pale face twisted into a smile that suggested that to see the chaise was not merely a pleasure to him, but actually a joy so sweet as to be painful.

'Oh dear! oh dear!' he began in a thin sing-song voice, breathless, fussing about and preventing the travellers from getting out of the chaise by his antics. 'What a happy day for me! Oh, what am I to do now? Ivan Ivanitch! Father Christopher! What a pretty little gentleman sitting on the box, God strike me dead! Oh, my goodness! why am I standing here instead of asking the visitors indoors? Please walk in, I humbly beg you. . . . You are kindly welcome! Give me all your things. . . . Oh, my goodness me!'

Moisey Moisevitch, who was rummaging in the chaise and assisting the travellers to alight, suddenly turned back and shouted in a voice as frantic and choking as though he were drowning and calling for help:

'Solomon! Solomon!'

'Solomon! Solomon!' a woman's voice repeated indoors.

The swing-door creaked, and in the doorway appeared a rather short young Jew with a big beak-like nose, with a bald patch surrounded by rough red curly hair; he was dressed in a short and very shabby reefer jacket, with rounded lappets and short sleeves, and in short serge trousers, so that he looked skimpy and short-tailed like an unfledged bird. This was Solomon, the brother of Moisey Moisevitch. He went up to the chaise, smiling rather queerly, and did not speak or greet the travellers.

'Ivan Ivanitch and Father Christopher have come,' said Moisey Moisevitch in a tone as though he were afraid his brother would not believe him. 'Dear, dear! What a surprise! Such honoured guests to have come to us so suddenly! Come, take their things, Solomon. Walk in, honoured guests.'

A little later Kuzmitchov, Father Christopher, and Yegorushka were sitting in a big gloomy empty room at an old oak table. The table was almost in solitude, for, except a wide sofa covered with torn American leather and three chairs, there was no other furniture in the room. And, indeed, not everybody would have given the chairs that name. They were a pitiful semblance of furniture, covered with American leather that had seen its best days, and with backs bent backwards at an unnaturally acute angle, so that they looked like children's sledges. It was hard to imagine what had been the unknown carpenter's object in bending the chair-backs so mercilessly, and one was tempted to imagine that it was not the carpenter's fault, but that some athletic visitor had bent the

chairs like this as a feat, then had tried to bend them back again
and had made them worse. The room looked gloomy, the
walls were grey, the ceilings and the cornices were grimy; on
the floor were chinks and yawning holes that were hard to
account for (one might have fancied they were made by the
heel of the same athlete), and it seemed as though the room
would still have been dark if a dozen lamps had hung in it.
There was nothing approaching an ornament on the walls or
the windows. On one wall, however, there hung a list of
regulations of some sort under a two-headed eagle in a grey
wooden frame, and on another wall in the same sort of frame
an engraving with the inscription, "The Indifference of Man".
What it was to which men were indifferent it was impossible
to make out, as the engraving was very dingy with age and
was extensively flyblown. There was a smell of something
decayed and sour in the room.

As he led the visitors into the room, Moisey Moisevitch
went on wriggling, gesticulating, shrugging and uttering
joyful exclamations; he considered these antics necessary in
order to seem polite and agreeable.

'When did our waggons go by?' Kuzmitchov asked.

'One party went by early this morning, and the other, Ivan
Ivanitch, put up here for dinner and went on towards evening.'

'Ah! . . . Has Varlamov been by or not?'

'No, Ivan Ivanitch. His clerk, Grigory Yegoritch, went by
yesterday morning and said that he had to be today at the
Molokan's farm.'

'Good! so we will go after the waggons directly and then on
to the Molokans'.'

'Mercy on us, Ivan Ivanitch!' Moisey Moisevitch cried in
horror, flinging up his hands. 'Where are you going for the
night? You will have a nice little supper and stay the night, and
to-morrow morning, please God, you can go on and overtake
anyone you like.'

'There is no time for that. . . . Excuse me, Moisey
Moisevitch, another time; but now I must make haste. We'll
stay a quarter of an hour and then go on; we can stay the night
at the Molokans'.'

'A quarter of an hour!' squealed Moisey Moisevitch. 'Have
you no fear of God, Ivan Ivanitch? You will compel me to hide

your caps and lock the door! You must have a cup of tea and a snack of something, anyway.'

'We have no time for tea,' said Kuzmitchov.

Moisey Moisevitch bent his head on one side, crooked his knees, and put his open hands before him as though warding off a blow, while with a smile of agonized sweetness he began imploring:

'Ivan Ivanitch! Father Christopher! Do be so good as to take a cup of tea with me. Surely I am not such a bad man that you can't even drink tea in my house? Ivan Ivanitch!'

'Well, we may just as well have a cup of tea,' said Father Christopher, with a sympathetic smile; 'that won't keep us long.'

'Very well,' Kuzmitchov assented.

Moisey Moisevitch, in a fluster uttered an exclamation of joy, and shrugging as though he had just stepped out of cold water into warm, ran to the door and cried in the same frantic voice in which he had called Solomon:

'Rosa! Rosa! Bring the samovar!'

A minute later the door opened, and Solomon came into the room carrying a large tray in his hands. Setting the tray on the table, he looked away sarcastically with the same queer smile as before. Now, by the light of the lamp, it was possible to see his smile distinctly; it was very complex, and expressed a variety of emotions, but the predominant element in it was undisguised contempt. He seemed to be thinking of something ludicrous and silly, to be feeling contempt and dislike, to be pleased at something and waiting for the favourable moment to turn something into ridicule and to burst into laughter. His long nose, his thick lips, and his sly prominent eyes seemed tense with the desire to laugh. Looking at his face, Kuzmitchov smiled ironically and asked:

'Solomon, why did you not come to our fair at N. this summer, and act some Jewish scenes?'

Two years before, as Yegorushka remembered very well, at one of the booths at the fair at N., Solomon had performed some scenes of Jewish life, and his acting had been a great success. The allusion to this made no impression whatever upon Solomon. Making no answer, he went out and returned a little later with the samovar.

When he had done what he had to do at the table he moved a little aside, and, folding his arms over his chest and thrusting out one leg, fixed his sarcastic eyes on Father Christopher. There was something defiant, haughty, and contemptuous in his attitude, and at the same time it was comic and pitiful in the extreme, because the more impressive his attitude the more vividly it showed up his short trousers, his bobtail coat, his caricature of a nose, and his bird-like plucked-looking little figure.

Moisey Moisevitch brought a footstool from the other room and sat down a little way from the table.

'I wish you a good appetite! Tea and sugar!' he began, trying to entertain his visitors. 'I hope you will enjoy it. Such rare guests, such rare ones; it is years since I last saw Father Christopher. And will no one tell me who is this nice little gentleman?' he asked, looking tenderly at Yegorushka.

'He is the son of my sister, Olga Ivanovna,' answered Kuzmitchov.

'And where is he going?'

'To school. We are taking him to a high school.'

In his politeness, Moisey Moisevitch put on a look of wonder and wagged his head expressively.

'Ah, that is a fine thing,' he said, shaking his finger at the samovar. 'That's a fine thing. You will come back from the high school such a gentleman that we shall all take off our hats to you. You will be wealthy and wise and so grand that your mamma will be delighted. Oh, that's a fine thing!'

He paused a little, stroked his knees, and began again in a jocose and deferential tone.

'You must excuse me, Father Christopher, but I am thinking of writing to the bishop to tell him you are robbing the merchants of their living. I shall take a sheet of stamped paper and write that I suppose Father Christopher is short of pence, as he has taken up with trade and begun selling wool.'

'H'm, yes . . . it's a queer notion in my old age,' said Father Christopher, and he laughed. 'I have turned from priest to merchant, brother. I ought to be at home now saying my prayers, instead of galloping about the country like a Pharaoh in his chariot. . . . Vanity!'

'But it will mean a lot of pence!'

'Oh, I dare say! More kicks than halfpence, and serve me right. The wool's not mine, but my son-in-law Mihail's!'

'Why doesn't he go himself?'

'Why, because . . . His mother's milk is scarcely dry upon his lips. He can buy wool all right, but when it comes to selling, he has no sense; he is young yet. He has wasted all his money; he wanted to grow rich and cut a dash, but he tried here and there, and no one would give him his price. And so the lad went on like that for a year, and then he came to me and said "Daddy, you sell the wool for me; be kind and do it! I am no good at the business!" And that is true enough. As soon as there is anything wrong then it's "Daddy," but till then they could get on without their dad. When he was buying he did not consult me, but now when he is in difficulties it's Daddy's turn. And what does his dad know about it? If it were not for Ivan Ivanitch, his dad could do nothing. I have a lot of worry with them.'

'Yes, one has a lot of worry with one's children, I can tell you that,' sighed Moisey Moisevitch. 'I have six of my own. One needs schooling, another needs doctoring, and a third needs nursing, and when they grow up they are more trouble still. It is not only nowadays, it was the same in Holy Scripture. When Jacob had little children he wept, and when they grew up he wept still more bitterly.'

'H'm, yes . . . ' Father Christopher assented pensively, looking at his glass. 'I have no cause myself to rail against the Lord. I have lived to the end of my days as any man might be thankful to live. . . . I have married my daughters to good men, my sons I have set up in life, and now I am free; I have done my work and can go where I like. I live in peace with my wife. I eat and drink and sleep and rejoice in my grandchildren, and say my prayers and want nothing more. I live on the fat of the land, and don't need to curry favour with anyone. I have never had any trouble from childhood, and now suppose the Tsar were to ask me, 'What do you need? What would you like?' why, I don't need anything, I have everything I want and everything to be thankful for. In the whole town there is no happier man than I am. My only trouble is I have so many sins, but there – only God is without sin. That's right, isn't it?'

'No doubt it is.'

'I have no teeth, of course; my poor old back aches; there is one thing and another. . . . asthma and that sort of thing. . . . I ache. . . . The flesh is weak, but then think of my age! I am in the eighties! One can't go on for ever; one mustn't outstay one's welcome.'

Father Christopher suddenly thought of something, spluttered into his glass and choked with laughter. Moisey Moisevitch laughed, too, from politeness, and he, too, cleared his throat.

'So funny!' said Father Christopher, and he waved his hand. 'My eldest son Gavrila came to pay me a visit. He is in the medical line, and is a district doctor in the province of Tchernigov. . . . "Very well . . ." I said to him, "here I have asthma and one thing and another. . . . You are a doctor; cure your father!" He undressed me on the spot, tapped me, listened, and all sorts of tricks. . . . kneaded my stomach, and then he said, "Dad, you ought to be treated with compressed air". Father Christopher laughed convulsively, till the tears came into his eyes, and got up.

'And I said to him, "God bless your compressed air!"' he brought out through his laughter, waving both hands. "God bless your compressed air!"'

Moisey Moisevitch got up, too, and with his hands on his stomach, went off into shrill laughter like the yap of a lap-dog.

'God bless the compressed air!' repeated Father Christopher, laughing.

Moisey Moisevitch laughed two notes higher and so violently that he could hardly stand on his feet.

'Oh dear!' he moaned through his laughter. 'Let me get my breath. . . . You'll be the death of me.'

He laughed and talked, though at the same time he was casting timorous and suspicious looks at Solomon. The latter was standing in the same attitude and still smiling. To judge from his eyes and his smile, his contempt and hatred were genuine, but that was so out of keeping with his plucked-looking figure that it seemed to Yegorushka as though he were putting on his defiant attitude and biting sarcastic smile to play the fool for the entertainment of their honoured guests.

After drinking six glasses of tea in silence, Kuzmitchov

cleared a space before him on the table, took his bag, the one which he kept under his head when he slept under the chaise, untied the string and shook it. Rolls of paper notes were scattered out of the bag on the table.

'While we have the time, Father Christopher, let us reckon up,' said Kuzmitchov.

Moisey Moisevitch was embarrassed at the sight of the money. He got up, and, as a man of delicate feeling unwilling to pry into other people's secrets, he went out of the room on tiptoe, swaying his arms. Solomon remained where he was.

'How many are there in the rolls of roubles?' Father Christopher began.

'The rouble notes are done up in fifties. . . . the three-rouble notes in nineties, the twenty-five and hundred roubles in thousands. You count out seven thousand eight hundred for Varlamov, and I will count out for Gusevitch. And mind you don't make a mistake. . . .'

Yegorushka had never in his life seen so much money as was lying on the table before him. There must have been a great deal of money, for the roll of seven thousand eight hundred, which Father Christopher put aside for Varlamov, seemed very small compared with the whole heap. At any other time such a mass of money would have impressed Yegorushka, and would have moved him to reflect how many cracknels, buns and poppy-cakes could be bought for that money. Now he looked at it listlessly, only conscious of the disgusting smell of kerosene and rotten apples that came from the heap of notes. He was exhausted by the jolting ride in the chaise, tired out and sleepy. His head was heavy, his eyes would hardly keep open and his thoughts were tangled like threads. If it had been possible he would have been relieved to lay his head on the table, so as not to see the lamp and the fingers moving over the heaps of notes, and to have let his tired sleepy thoughts go still more at random. When he tried to keep awake, the light of the lamp, the cups and the fingers grew double, the samovar heaved and the smell of rotten apples seemed even more acrid and disgusting.

'Ah, money, money!' sighed Father Christopher, smiling. 'You bring trouble! Now I expect my Mihailo is asleep and dreaming that I am going to bring him a heap of money like this.'

'Your Mihailo Timofevitch is a man who doesn't understand business,' said Kuzmitchov in an undertone; 'he undertakes what isn't his work, but you understand and can judge. You had better hand over your wool to me, as I have said already, and I would give you half a rouble above my own price – yes, I would, simply out of regard for you . . . .'

'No, Ivan Ivanitch,' Father Christopher sighed. 'I thank you for your kindness . . . . Of course, if it were for me to decide, I shouldn't think twice about it; but as it is, the wool is not mine, as you know . . . .'

Moisey Moisevitch came in on tiptoe. Trying from delicacy not to look at the heaps of money, he stole up to Yegorushka and pulled at his shirt from behind.

'Come along, little gentleman,' he said in an undertone, 'come and see the little bear I can show you! Such a queer cross little bear. Oo-oo!'

The sleepy boy got up and listlessly dragged himself after Moisey Moisevitch to see the bear. He went into a little room, where, before he saw anything, he felt he could not breathe from the smell of something sour and decaying, which was much stronger here than in the big room and probably spread from this room all over the house. One part of the room was occupied by a big bed, covered with a greasy quilt and another by a chest of drawers and heaps of rags of all kinds from a woman's stiff petticoat to children's little breeches and braces. A tallow candle stood on the chest of drawers.

Instead of the promised bear, Yegorushka saw a big fat Jewess with her hair hanging loose, in a red flannel skirt with black sprigs on it; she turned with difficulty in the narrow space between the bed and the chest of drawers and uttered drawn-out moaning as though she had toothache. On seeing Yegorushka, she made a doleful, woe-begone face, heaved a long-drawn-out sigh, and before he had time to look round, put to his lips a slice of bread smeared with honey.

'Eat it, dearie, eat it!' she said. 'You are here without your mamma, and no one to look after you. Eat it up.'

Yegorushka did eat it, though after the goodies and poppy-cakes he had every day at home, he did not think very much of the honey, which was mixed with wax and bees' wings. He ate while Moisey Moisevitch and the Jewess looked at him and sighed.

'Where are you going, dearie?' asked the Jewess.

'To school,' answered Yegorushka.

'And how many brothers and sisters have you got?'

'I am the only one; there are no others.'

'O-oh!' sighed the Jewess, and turned her eyes upward. 'Poor mamma, poor mamma! How she will weep and miss you! We are going to send our Nahum to school in a year. O-oh!'

'Ah, Nahum, Nahum!' sighed Moisey Moisevitch, and the skin of his pale face twitched nervously. 'And he is so delicate.'

The greasy quilt quivered, and from beneath it appeared a child's curly head on a very thin neck; two black eyes gleamed and stared with curiosity at Yegorushka. Still sighing, Moisey Moisevitch and the Jewess went to the chest of drawers and began talking in Yiddish. Moisey Moisevitch spoke in a low bass undertone, and altogether his talk in Yiddish was like a continual 'ghaal-ghaal-ghaal-ghaal. . . .' while his wife answered him in a shrill voice like a turkeycock's, and the whole effect of her talk was something like 'Too-too-too-too!' While they were consulting, another little curly head on a thin neck peeped out of the greasy quilt, then a third, then a fourth . . .

If Yegorushka had had a fertile imagination he might have imagined that the hundred-headed hydra was hiding under the quilt.

'Ghaal-ghaal-ghaal-ghaal!' said Moisey Moisevitch.

'Too-too-too-too!' answered the Jewess.

The consultation ended in the Jewess's diving with a deep sigh into the chest of drawers, and, unwrapping some sort of green rag there, she took out a big rye cake made in the shape of a heart.

'Take it dearie,' she said, giving Yegorushka the cake; 'you have no mamma now – no one to give you nice things.'

Yegorushka stuck the cake in his pocket and staggered to the door, as he could not go on breathing the foul, sour air in which the innkeeper and his wife lived. Going back to the big room, he settled himself more comfortably on the sofa and gave up trying to check his straying thoughts.

As soon as Kuzmitchov had finished counting out the notes he put them back into the bag. He did not treat them very respectfully and stuffed them into the dirty sack without ceremony, as indifferently as though they had not been money but waste paper.

Father Christopher was talking to Solomon.

'Well, Solomon the Wise!' he said, yawning and making the sign of the cross over his mouth. 'How is business?'

'What sort of business are you talking about?' asked Solomon, and he looked as fiendish, as though it were a hint of some sort of crime on his part.

'Oh, things in general. What are you doing?'

'What am I doing?' Solomon repeated, and he shrugged his shoulders. 'The same as everyone else. . . . You see, I am a menial, I am my brother's servant; my brother's the servant of the visitors; the visitors are Varlamov's servants; and if I had ten millions, Varlamov would be my servant.'

'Why would he be your servant?'

'Why, because there isn't a gentleman or millionaire who isn't ready to lick the hand of a scabby Jew for the sake of making a kopeck. Now, I am a scabby Jew and a beggar. Everybody looks at me as though I were a dog, but if I had money Varlamov would play the fool before me just as Moisey does before you.'

Father Christopher and Kuzmitchov looked at each other. Neither of them understood Solomon. Kuzmitchov looked at him sternly and dryly, and asked:

'How can you compare yourself with Varlamov, you blockhead?'

'I am not such a fool as to put myself on a level with Varlamov,' answered Solomon, looking sarcastically at the speaker. 'Though Varlamov is a Russian, he is at heart a scabby Jew; money and gain are all he lives for, but I threw my money in the stove! I don't want money, or land, or sheep, and there is no need for people to be afraid of me and to take off their hats when I pass. So I am wiser than your Varlamov and more like a man!'

A little later Yegorushka, half asleep, heard Solomon in a hoarse hollow voice choked with hatred, in hurried stuttering phrases, talking about the Jews. At first he talked correctly in

Russian, then he fell into the tone of a Jewish recitation, and began speaking as he had done at the fair with an exaggerated Jewish accent.

'Stop! . . .' Father Christopher said to him. 'If you don't like your religion you had better change it, but to laugh at it is a sin; it is only the lowest of the low who will make fun of his religion.'

You don't understand,' Solomon cut him short rudely. 'I am talking of one thing and you are talking of something else . . .'

'One can see you are a foolish fellow,' sighed Father Christopher. 'I admonish you to the best of my ability, and you are angry. I speak to you like an old man quietly, and you answer like a turkeycock: "Bla-bla-bla!" You really are a queer fellow.'

Moisey Moisevitch came in. He looked anxiously at Solomon and at his visitors, and again the skin on his face quivered nervously. Yegorushka shook his head and looked about him; he caught a passing glimpse of Solomon's face at the very moment when it was turned three-quarters towards him and when the shadow of his long nose divided his left cheek in half; the contemptuous smile mingled with that shadow; the gleaming sarcastic eyes, the haughty expression, and the whole plucked-looking little figure, dancing and doubling itself before Yegorushka's eyes, made him now not like a buffoon, but like something one sometimes dreams of, like an evil spirit.

'What a ferocious fellow you've got here, Moisey Moisevitch! God bless him!' said Father Christopher with a smile. 'You ought to find him a place or a wife or something. . . . There's no knowing what to make of him. . . .'

Kuzmitchov frowned angrily. Moisey Moisevitch looked uneasily and inquiringly at his brother and the visitors again.

'Solomon, go away!' he said shortly. 'Go away!' and he added something in Yiddish. Solomon gave an abrupt laugh and went out.

'What was it?' Moisey Moisevitch asked Father Christopher anxiously.

'He forgets himself,' answered Kuzmitchov. 'He's rude and thinks too much of himself.'

'I knew it!' Moisey Moisevitch cried in horror, clasping his hands. 'Oh dear, oh dear!' he muttered in a low voice. 'Be so kind as to excuse it, and don't be angry. He is such a queer fellow, such a queer fellow! Oh dear, oh dear! He is my own brother, but I have never had anything but trouble from him. You know he's . . .'

Moisey Moisevitch crooked his finger by his forehead and went on:

'He is not in his right mind; . . . he's hopeless. And I don't know what I am to do with him! He cares for nobody, he respects nobody, and is afraid of nobody. . . . You know he laughs at everybody, he says silly things, speaks familiarly to anyone. You wouldn't believe it, Varlamov came here one day and Solomon said such things to him that he gave us both a taste of his whip. . . . But why whip me? Was it my fault? God has robbed him of his wits, so it is God's will, and how am I to blame?'

Ten minutes passed and Moisey Moisevitch was still muttering in an undertone and sighing:

'He does not sleep at night, and is always thinking and thinking and thinking, and what he is thinking about God only knows. If you go to him at night he is angry and laughs. He doesn't like me either. . . . And there is nothing he wants! When our father died he left us each six thousand roubles. I bought myself an inn, married, and now I have children; and he burnt all his money in the stove. Such a pity, such a pity! Why burn it? If he didn't want it he could give it to me, but why burn it?'

Suddenly the swing-door creaked and the floor shook under footsteps. Yegorushka felt a draught of cold air, and it seemed to him as though some big black bird had passed by him and had fluttered its wings close in his face. He opened his eyes . . . . His uncle was standing by the sofa with his sack in his hands ready for departure; Father Christopher, holding his broad-brimmed top-hat, was bowing to someone and smiling – not his usual soft kindly smile, but a respectful forced smile which did not suit his face at all – while Moisey Moisevitch looked as though his body had been broken into three parts, and he were balancing and doing his utmost not to drop to pieces. Only Solomon stood in the corner with his arms folded, as though nothing had happened, and smiled contemptuously as before.

'Your Excellency must excuse us for not being tidy,' moaned Moisey Moisevitch with the agonizingly sweet smile, taking no more notice of Kuzmitchov or Father Christopher, but swaying his whole person so as to avoid dropping to pieces. 'We are plain folks, your Excellency.'

Yegorushka rubbed his eyes. In the middle of the room there really was standing an Excellency, in the form of a young plump and very beautiful woman in a black dress and a straw hat. Before Yegorushka had time to examine her features the image of the solitary graceful poplar he had seen that day on the hill for some reason came into his mind.

'Has Varlamov been here today?' a woman's voice inquired.

'No, your Excellency,' said Moisey Moisevitch.

'If you see him tomorrow, ask him to come and see me for a minute.'

All at once, quite unexpectedly, Yegorushka saw half an inch from his eyes velvety black eyebrows, big brown eyes, delicate feminine cheeks with dimples, from which smiles seemed radiating all over the face like sunbeams. There was a glorious scent.

'What a pretty boy!' said the lady. 'Whose boy is it? Kazimir Mihalovitch, look what a charming fellow! Good heavens, he is asleep!'

And the lady kissed Yegorushka warmly on both cheeks, and he smiled and, thinking he was asleep, shut his eyes. The swing-door squeaked, and there was the sound of hurried footsteps, coming in and going out.

'Yegorushka, Yegorushka!' he heard two bass voices whisper. 'Get up; it is time to start.'

Somebody, it seemed to be Deniska, set him on his feet and led him by the arm. On the way he half-opened his eyes and once more saw the beautiful lady in the black dress who had kissed him. She was standing in the middle of the room and watched him go out, smiling at him and nodding her head in a friendly way. As he got near the door he saw a handsome, stoutly built, dark man in a bowler hat and in leather gaiters. This must have been the lady's escort.

'Woa!' he heard from the yard.

At the front door Yegorushka saw a splendid new carriage and a pair of black horses. On the box sat a groom in livery, with a long whip in his hands. No one but Solomon came to see the travellers off. His face was tense with a desire to laugh; he looked as though he were waiting impatiently for the visitors to be gone, so that he might laugh at them without restraint.

'The Countess Dranitsky,' whispered Father Christopher, clambering into the chaise.

'Yes, Countess Dranitsky,' repeated Kuzmitchov, also in a whisper.

The impression made by the arrival of the countess was probably very great, for even Deniska spoke in a whisper, and only ventured to lash his bays and shout when the chaise had driven a quarter of a mile away and nothing could be seen of the inn but a dim light.

CHAPTER IV

Who was this elusive, mysterious Varlamov of whom people talked so much, whom Solomon despised, and whom even the beautiful countess needed? Sitting on the box beside Deniska, Yegorushka, half asleep, thought about this person. He had never seen him. But he had often heard of him and pictured him in his imagination. He knew that Varlamov possessed several tens of thousands of acres of land, about a hundred thousand sheep, and a great deal of money. Of his manner of life and occupation Yegorushka knew nothing, except that he was always 'going his rounds in these parts', and he was always being looked for.

At home Yegorushka had heard a great deal of the Countess Dranitsky, too. She, too, had some tens of thousands of acres, a great many sheep, a stud farm and a great deal of money, but she did not 'go rounds', but lived at home in a splendid house and grounds, about which Ivan Ivanitch, who had been more than once at the countess's on business, and other acquaintances told many marvellous tales; thus, for instance, they said that in the countess's drawing-room, where the portraits of all the kings of Poland hung on the walls, there was a big table-clock in the form of a rock, on the rock a gold horse with diamond eyes, rearing, and on the horse the figure of a rider also of gold, who brandished his sword to right and to left whenever the clock struck. They said, too, that twice a year the countess used to give a ball, to which the gentry and officials of the whole province were invited, and to which even Varlamov used to come; all the visitors drank tea from silver samovars, ate all sorts of extraordinary things (they had strawberries and raspberries, for instance, in winter at Christmas), and danced to a band which played day and night. . . .

'And how beautiful she is,' thought Yegorushka, remembering her face and smile.

Kuzmitchov, too, was probably thinking about the

countess. For when the chaise had driven a mile and a half he said:

'But doesn't that Kazimir Mihalovitch plunder her right and left! The year before last when, do you remember, I bought some wool from her, he made over three thousand from my purchase alone.'

'That is just what you would expect from a Pole,' said Father Christopher.

'And little does it trouble her. Young and foolish, as they say, her head is full of nonsense.'

Yegorushka, for some reason, longed to think of nothing but Varlamov and the countess, particularly the latter. His drowsy brain utterly refused ordinary thoughts, was in a cloud and retained only fantastic fairy-tale images, which have the advantage of springing into the brain of themselves without any effort on the part of the thinker, and completely vanishing of themselves at a mere shake of the head; and, indeed, nothing that was around him disposed to ordinary thoughts. On the right there were the dark hills which seemed to be screening something unseen and terrible; on the left the whole sky about the horizon was covered with a crimson glow, and it was hard to tell whether there was a fire somewhere, or whether it was the moon about to rise. As by day the distance could be seen, but its tender lilac tint had gone, quenched by the evening darkness, in which the whole steppe was hidden like Moisey Moisevitch's children under the quilt.

Corncrakes and quails do not call in the July nights, the nightingale does not sing in the woodland marsh, and there is no scent of flowers, but still the steppe is lovely and full of life. As soon as the sun goes down and the darkness enfolds the earth, the day's weariness is forgotten, everything is forgiven, and the steppe breathes a light sigh from its broad bosom. As though because the grass cannot see in the dark that it has grown old, a gay youthful twitter rises up from it, such as is not heard by day; chirruping, twittering, whistling, scratching, the basses, tenors and sopranos of the steppe all mingle in an incessant, monotonous roar of sound in which it is sweet to brood on memories and sorrows. The monotonous twitter soothes to sleep like a lullaby; you drive and feel you are falling asleep, but suddenly there comes the abrupt agitated cry of a wakeful bird, or a vague sound like a voice crying out in wonder "A-ah, a-ah!" and slumber closes one's eyelids again. Or you drive by a little creek where there are bushes and hear the bird, called by the steppe dwellers "the sleeper", call "Asleep, asleep, asleep!" while another laughs or breaks into trills of hysterical weeping – that is the owl. For whom do they call and who hears them on that plain, God only knows, but there is deep sadness and lamentation in their cry. . . . There is a scent of hay and dry grass and belated flowers, but the scent is heavy, sweetly mawkish and soft.

Everything can be seen through the mist, but it is hard to make out the colours and the outlines of objects. Everything looks different from what it is. You drive on and suddenly see standing before you right in the roadway a dark figure like a monk; it stands motionless, waiting, holding something in its hands. . . . Can it be a robber? The figure comes closer, grows bigger; now it is on a level with the chaise, and you see it is not a man, but a solitary bush or a great stone. Such motionless expectant figures stand on the low hills, hide behind the old barrows, peep out from the high grass, and they all look like human beings and arouse suspicion.

And when the moon rises the night becomes pale and dim. The mist seems to have passed away. The air is transparent, fresh and warm; one can see well in all directions and even distinguish the separate stalks of grass by the wayside. Stones and bits of pots can be seen at a long distance. The suspicious figures like monks look blacker against the light background of the night, and seem more sinister. More and more often in the midst of the monotonous chirruping there comes the sound of the "A-ah, a-ah!" of astonishment troubling the motionless air, and the cry of a sleepless or delirious bird. Broad shadows move across the plain like clouds across the sky, and in the inconceivable distance, if you look long and intently at it, misty monstrous shapes rise up and huddle one against another. . . . It is rather uncanny. One glances at the pale green, star-spangled sky on which there is no cloudlet, no spot, and understands why the warm air is motionless, why nature is on her guard, afraid to stir: she is afraid and reluctant to lose one instant of life. Of the unfathomable depth and infinity of the sky one can only form a conception at sea and on the steppe by night when the moon is shining. It is terribly lonely and caressing; it looks down languid and alluring, and its caressing sweetness makes one giddy.

You drive on for one hour, for a second. . . . You meet upon the way a silent old barrow or a stone figure put up God knows when and by whom; a nightbird floats noiselessly over the earth, and little by little those legends of the steppes, the tales of men you have met, the stories of some old nurse from the steppe, and all the things you have managed to see and treasure in your soul, come back to your mind. And then in the churring of insects, in the sinister figures, in the ancient barrows, in the blue sky, in the moonlight, in the flight of the nightbird, in everything you see and hear, triumphant beauty, youth, the fullness of power, and the passionate thirst for life begin to be apparent; the soul responds to the call of her lovely austere fatherland, and longs to fly over the steppes with the nightbird. And in the triumph of beauty, in the exuberance of happiness you are conscious of yearning and grief, as though the steppe knew she was solitary, knew that her wealth and her inspiration were wasted for the world, not glorified in song, not wanted by anyone; and through the joyful clamour one hears her mournful, hopeless call for singers, singers!

'Woa! Good-evening, Panteley! Is everything all right?'

'First-rate, Ivan Ivanvitch!'

'Haven't you seen Varlamov, lads?'

'No, we haven't.'

Yegorushka woke up and opened his eyes. The chaise had stopped. On the right the train of waggons stretched for a long way ahead on the road, and men were moving to and fro near them. All the waggons being loaded up with great bales of wool looked very high and fat, while the horses looked short-legged and little.

'Well, then, we shall go on to the Molokans'!' Kuzmitchov said aloud. 'The Jew told us that Varlamov was putting up for the night at the Molokans'. So good-bye, lads! Good luck to you!'

'Good-bye, Ivan Ivanitch,' several voices replied.

'I say, lads,' Kuzmitchov cried briskly, 'you take my little lad along with you! Why should he go jolting off with us for nothing? You put him on the bales, Panteley, and let him come on slowly, and we shall overtake you. Get down, Yegor! Go on; it's all right. . . .'

Yegorushka got down from the box-seat. Several hands caught him, lifted him high into the air, and he found himself on something big, soft, and rather wet with dew. It seemed to him now as though the sky were quite close and the earth far away.

'Hey, take his little coat!' Deniska shouted from somewhere far below.

His coat and bundle flung up from far below fell close to Yegorushka. Anxious not to think of anything, he quickly put his bundle under his head and covered himself with his coat, and stretching his legs out and shrinking a little from the dew, he laughed with content.

'Sleep, sleep, sleep. . . .' he thought.

'Don't be unkind to him, you devils!' he heard Deniska's voice below.

'Good-bye lads; good luck to you,' shouted Kuzmitchov. 'I rely upon you!'

'Don't you be uneasy, Ivan Ivanitch!'

Deniska shouted to the horses, the chaise creaked and started, not along the road, but somewhere off to the side. For two minutes there was silence, as though the waggons were asleep and there was no sound except the clanking of the pails tied on at the back of the chaise as it slowly died away in the distance. Then someone at the head of the waggons shouted:

'Kiruha! Sta-art!'

The foremost of the waggons creaked, then the second, then the third. . . . Yegorushka felt the waggon he was on sway and creak also. The waggons were moving. Yegorushka took a tighter hold of the cord with which the bales were tied on, laughed again with content, shifted the cake in his pocket, and fell asleep just as he did in his bed at home. . . .

When he woke up the sun had risen, it was screened by an ancient barrow, and, trying to shed its light upon the earth, it scattered its beams in all directions and flooded the horizon with gold. It seemed to Yegorushka that it was not in its proper place, as the day before it had risen behind his back, and now it was much more to his left. . . . And the whole landscape was different. There were no hills now, but on all sides, wherever one looked, there stretched the brown cheerless plain; here and there upon it small barrows rose up and rooks flew as they had done the day before. The belfries and huts of some village showed white in the distance ahead; as it was Sunday the Little Russians were at home baking and cooking – that could be seen by the smoke which rose from every chimney and hung, a dark blue transparent veil, over the village. In between the huts and beyond the church there were blue glimpses of a river, and beyond the river a misty distance. But nothing was so different from yesterday as the road. Something extraordinarily broad, spread out and titanic, stretched over the steppe by way of a road. It was a grey streak well trodden down and covered with dust, like all roads. Its width puzzled Yegorushka and brought thoughts of fairy tales to his mind. Who travelled along that road? Who needed so much space? It was strange and unintelligible. It might have been supposed that giants with immense strides, such as Ilya Muromets and Solovy the Brigand, were still surviving in Russia, and that their gigantic steeds were still alive. Yegorushka, looking at the road, imagined some half a dozen high chariots racing along side by side, like some he used to see in pictures in his Scripture history; these chariots were each drawn by six wild furious horses, and their great wheels raised a cloud of dust to the sky, while the horses were driven by men such as one may see in one's dreams or in imagination brooding over fairy tales. And if those figures had existed, how perfectly in keeping with the steppe and the road they would have been!

Telegraph-poles with two wires on them stretched along the right side of the road to its furthermost limit. Growing smaller and smaller, they disappeared near the village behind the huts and green trees, and then again came into sight in the lilac distance in the form of very small thin sticks that looked like pencils stuck into the ground. Hawks, falcons, and crows sat on the wires and looked indifferently at the moving waggons.

Yegorushka was lying in the last of the waggons, and so could see the whole string. There were about twenty waggons, and there was a driver to every three waggons. By the last waggon, the one in which Yegorushka was, there walked an old man with a grey beard, as short and lean as Father Christopher, but with a sunburnt, stern and brooding face. It is very possible that the old man was not stern and not brooding, but his red eyelids and his sharp long nose gave his face a stern frigid expression such as is common with people in the habit of continually thinking of serious things in solitude. Like Father Christopher he was wearing a wide-brimmed top-hat, not like a gentleman's, but made of brown felt, and in shape more like a cone with the top cut off than a real top-hat. Probably from a habit acquired in cold winters, when he must more than once have been nearly frozen as he trudged beside the waggons, he kept slapping his thighs and stamping with his feet as he walked. Noticing that Yegorushka was awake, he looked at him and said, shrugging his shoulders as though from the cold:

'Ah, you are awake, youngster! So you are the son of Ivan Ivanitch?'

'No; his nephew. . . .'

'Nephew of Ivan Ivanitch? Here I have taken off my boots and am hopping along barefoot. My feet are bad; they are swollen, and it's easier without my boots . . . easier, youngster . . . without boots, I mean. . . . So you are his nephew? He is a good man; no harm in him. . . . God give him health. . . . No harm in him . . . I mean Ivan Ivanitch. . . . He has gone to the Molokans'. . . . O Lord, have mercy upon us!'

The old man talked, too, as though it were very cold, pausing and not opening his mouth properly; and he mispronounced the labial consonants, stuttering over them as though his lips were frozen. As he talked to Yegorushka he did not once smile, and he seemed stern.

Two waggons ahead of them there walked a man wearing a long reddish-brown coat, a cap and high boots with sagging bootlegs, and carrying a whip in his hand. This was not an old man, only about forty. When he looked round Yegorushka saw a long red face with a scanty goat-beard and a spongy looking swelling under his right eye. Apart from this very ugly swelling, there was another peculiar thing about him which caught the eye at once: in his left hand he carried a whip, while he waved the right as though he were conducting an unseen choir; from time to time he put the whip under his arm, and then he conducted with both hands and hummed something to himself.

The next driver was a long rectilinear figure with extremely sloping shoulders and a back as flat as a board. He held himself as stiffly erect as though he were marching or had swallowed a yard measure. His hands did not swing as he walked, but hung down as if they were straight sticks, and he strode along in a wooden way, after the manner of toy soldiers, almost without bending his knees, and trying to take as long steps as possible. While the old man or the owner of the spongy swelling were taking two steps he succeeded in taking only one, and so it seemed as though he were walking more slowly than any of them, and would drop behind. His face was tied up in a rag, and on his head something stuck up that looked like a monk's peaked cap; he was dressed in a short Little Russian coat, with full dark blue trousers and bark shoes.

Yegorushka did not even distinguish those that were farther on. He lay on his stomach, picked a little hole in the bale, and, having nothing better to do, began twisting the wool into a thread. The old man trudging along below him turned out not to be so stern as one might have supposed from his face. Having begun a conversation, he did not let it drop.

'Where are you going?' he asked, stamping with his feet.

'To school,' answered Yegorushka.

'To school? Aha! . . . Well, may the Queen of Heaven help you. Yes. One brain is good, but two are better. To one man God gives one brain, to another two brains, and to another three. . . . To another three, that is true. . . . One brain you are born with, one you get from learning, and a third with a good life. So you see, my lad, it is a good thing if a man has three brains. Living is easier for him, and, what's more, dying is, too. Dying is, too. . . . And we shall all die for sure.'

The old man scratched his forehead, glanced upwards at Yegorushka with his red eyes, and went on:

'Maxim Nikolaitch, the gentleman from Slavyanoserbsk, brought a little lad to school, too, last year. I don't know how he is getting on there in studying the sciences, but he was a nice good little lad. . . . God give them help, they are nice

gentlemen. Yes, he, too, brought his boy to school. . . . In
Slavyanoserbsk there is no establishment, I suppose, for
study. No. . . . But it is a nice town. . . . There's an ordinary
school for simple folks, but for the higher studies there is
nothing. No, that's true. What's your name? . . .'

'Yegorushka.'

'Yegory, then. . . . The holy martyr Yegory, the Bearer of
Victory, whose day is the twenty-third of April. And my
christian name is Panteley. . . . Panteley Zaharov Hol-
odov. . . . We are Holodovs. . . . I am a native of – maybe
you've heard of it – Tim in the province of Kursk. My
brothers are artisans and work at trades in the town, but I am a
peasant. . . . I have remained a peasant. Seven years ago I
went there – home, I mean. I went to the village and to the
town. . . . To Tim, I mean. Then, thank God, they were all
alive and well. . . . but now I don't know. . . . Maybe some
of them are dead. . . . And it's time they did die, for some of
them are older than I am. Death is all right; it is good so long,
of course, as one does not die without repentance. There is no
worse evil than an impenitent death; an impenitent death is a
joy to the devil. And if you want to die penitent, so that you
may not be forbidden to enter the mansions of the Lord, pray
to the holy martyr Varvara. She is the intercessor. She is,
that's the truth. . . . For God has given her such a place in the
heavens that everyone has the right to pray to her for
penitence.'

Panteley went on muttering, and apparently did not trouble
whether Yegorushka heard him or not. He talked listlessly,
mumbling to himself, without raising or dropping his voice,
but succeeded in telling him a great deal in a short time. All he
said was made up of fragments that had very little connection
with one another, and quite uninteresting for Yegorushka.
Possibly he talked only in order to reckon over his thoughts
aloud after the night spent in silence, in order to see if they
were all there. After talking of repentance, he spoke about a
certain Maxim Nikolaitch from Slavyanoserbsk.

'Yes, he took his little lad. . . he took him, that's true.'

One of the waggoners walking in front darted from his
place, ran to one side and began lashing on the ground with his
whip. He was a stalwart, broad-shouldered man of thirty,

with curly flaxen hair and a look of great health and vigour. Judging from the movements of his shoulders and the whip, and the eagerness expressed in his attitude, he was beating something alive. Another waggoner, a short stubby little man with a bushy black beard, wearing a waistcoat and a shirt outside his trousers, ran up to him. The latter broke into a deep guffaw of laughter and coughing and said:

'I say, lads, Dymov has killed a snake!'

There are people whose intelligence can be gauged at once by their voice and laughter. The man with the black beard belonged to that class of fortunate individuals; impenetrable stupidity could be felt in his voice and laugh. The flaxen-headed Dymov had finished, and lifting from the ground with his whip something like a cord, flung it with a laugh into the cart.

'That's not a viper; it's a grass snake!' shouted someone.

The man with the wooden gait and the bandage round his face strode up quickly to the dead snake, glanced at it and flung up his stick-like arms.

'You jail-bird!' he cried in a hollow wailing voice. 'What have you killed a grass snake for? What had he done to you, you damned brute? Look, he has killed a grass snake; how would you like to be treated so?'

'Grass snakes ought not to be killed, that's true,' Panteley muttered placidly, 'they ought not. . . . They are not vipers; though it looks like a snake, it is a gentle, innocent creature. . . . It's friendly to man, the grass snake is.'

Dymov and the man with the black beard were probably ashamed, for they laughed loudly, and not answering, slouched lazily back to their waggons. When the hindmost waggon was level with the spot where the dead snake lay, the man with his face tied up standing over it turned to Panteley and asked in a tearful voice:

'Grandfather, what did he want to kill the grass snake for?'

His eyes, as Yegorushka saw now, were small and dingy looking; his face was grey, sickly and looked somehow dingy too while his chin was red and seemed very much swollen.

'Grandfather, what did he kill it for?' he repeated, striding along beside Panteley.

'A stupid fellow. His hands itch to kill, and that is why he does it,' answered the old man; 'but he oughtn't to kill a grass snake, that's true. . . . Dymov is a ruffian, we all know, he kills everything he comes across, and Kiruha did not interfere. He ought to have taken its part, but instead of that, he goes off into "Ha-ha-ha!" and "Ho-ho-ho!" . . . But don't be angry, Vassya. . . . Why be angry? They've killed it – well, never mind them. Dymov is a ruffian and Kiruha acted from foolishness – never mind. . . . They are foolish people without understanding – but there, don't mind them. Emelyan here never touches what he shouldn't. . . . he never does. . . . that is true. . . . because he is a man of education, while they are stupid. . . . Emelyan, he doesn't touch things.'

The waggoner in the reddish-brown coat and the spongy swelling on his face, who was conducting an unseen choir, stopped. Hearing his name, and waiting till Panteley and Vassya came up to him, he walked beside them.

'What are you talking about?' he asked in a husky muffled voice.

'Why, Vassya here is angry,' said Panteley. 'So I have been saying things to him to stop his being angry. . . . Oh, how my swollen feet hurt! Oh, oh! They are more inflamed than ever for Sunday, God's holy day!'

'It's from walking,' observed Vassya.

'No, lad, no. It's not from walking. When I walk it seems easier; when I lie down and get warm. . . . it's deadly. Walking is easier for me.'

Emelyan, in his reddish-brown coat, walked between Panteley and Vassya and waved his arms, as though they were going to sing. After waving them a little while he dropped them, and croaked out hopelessly:

'I have no voice. It's a real misfortune. All last night and this morning I have been haunted by the trio "Lord have Mercy" that we sang at the wedding at Marionovsky's. It's in my head and in my throat. It seems as though I could sing it, but can't; I have no voice.'

He paused for a minute, thinking, then went on:

'For fifteen years I was in the choir. In all the Lugansky works there was, maybe, no one with a voice like mine. But, confound it, I bathed two years ago in the Donets, and I can't get a single note true ever since. I took cold in my throat. And without a voice I am like a workman without hands.'

'That's true,' Panteley agreed.

'I think of myself as a ruined man and nothing more.'

At that moment Vassya chanced to catch sight of Yegorushka. His eyes grew moist and smaller than ever.

'There's a little gentleman driving with us,' and he covered his nose with his sleeve as though he were bashful. 'What a grand driver! Stay with us and you shall drive the waggons and sell wool.'

The incongruity of one person being at once a little gentleman and a waggon driver seemed to strike him as very queer and funny, for he burst into a loud guffaw, and went on enlarging upon the idea. Emelyan glanced upwards at Yegorushka, too, but coldly and cursorily. He was absorbed in his own thoughts, and had it not been for Vassya, would not have noticed Yegorushka's presence. Before five minutes had passed he was waving his arms again, then describing to his companions the beauties of the wedding anthem, 'Lord, have Mercy,' which he had remembered in the night. He put the whip under his arm and waved both hands.

A mile from the village the waggons stopped by a well with a crane. Letting his pail down into the well, black-bearded Kiruha lay on his stomach on the framework and thrust his shaggy head, his shoulders, and part of his chest into the black hole, so that Yegorushka could see nothing but his short legs, which scarcely touched the ground. Seeing the reflection of his head far down at the bottom of the well, he was delighted and went off into his deep bass stupid laugh, and the echo from the well answered him. When he got up his neck and face were as red as beetroot. The first to run up and drink was Dymov. He drank laughing, often turning from the pail to tell Kiruha something funny, then he turned round, and uttered aloud, to be heard all over the steppe, five very bad words. Yegorushka did not understand the meaning of such words, but he knew very well they were bad words. He knew the repulsion his friends and relations silently felt for such words. He himself, without knowing why, shared that feeling and was accustomed to think that only drunk and disorderly people enjoy the privilege of uttering such words aloud. He remembered the murder of the grass snake, listened to Dymov's laughter, and felt something like hatred for the man. And as ill-luck would have it, Dymov at that moment caught sight of Yegorushka, who had climbed down from the waggon and gone up to the well. He laughed aloud and shouted;

'I say, lads, the old man has been brought to bed of a boy in the night!'

Kiruha laughed his bass laugh till he coughed. Someone else laughed too, while Yegorushka crimsoned and made up his mind finally that Dymov was a very wicked man.

With his curly flaxen head, with his shirt opened on his chest and no hat on, Dymov looked handsome and exceptionally strong; in every movement he made one could see the reckless dare-devil and athlete, knowing his value. He shrugged his shoulders, put his arms akimbo, talked and laughed louder than any of the rest, and looked as though he were going to lift up something very heavy with one hand and astonish the whole world by doing so. His mischievous mocking eyes glided over the road, the waggons, and the sky without resting on anything, and seemed looking for someone to kill, just as a pastime, and something to laugh at. Evidently he was afraid of no one, would stick at nothing, and most likely was not in the least interested in Yegorushka's opinion of him. . . . Yegorushka meanwhile hated his flaxen head, his clear face, and his strength with his whole heart, listened with fear and loathing to his laughter, and kept thinking what word of abuse he could pay him out with.

Panteley, too, went up to the pail. He took out of his pocket a little green glass of an ikon lamp, wiped it with a rag, filled it from the pail and drank from it, then filled it again, wrapped the little glass in the rag, and then put it back into his pocket.

'Grandfather, why do you drink out of a lamp?' Yegorushka asked him, surprised.

'One man drinks out of a pail and another out of a lamp,' the old man answered evasively. 'Every man to his own taste. . . . You drink out of the pail – well, drink, and may it do you good. . . .'

'You darling, you beauty!' Vassya said suddenly, in a caressing plaintive voice. 'You darling!'

His eyes were fixed on the distance; they were moist and smiling, and his face wore the same expression as when he had looked at Yegorushka.

'Who is it you are talking to?' asked Kiruha.

'A darling fox. . . . lying on her back, playing like a dog.'

Everyone began staring into the distance, looking for the fox, but no one could see it, only Vassya with his grey muddy-looking eyes, and he was enchanted by it. His sight was extraordinarily keen, as Yegorushka learnt afterwards. He was so long-sighted that the brown steppe was for him always full of life and interest. He had only to look into the distance to see a fox, a hare, a bustard, or some other animal keeping at a distance from men. There was nothing strange in seeing a hare running away or a flying bustard – everyone crossing the steppes could see them; but it was not vouchsafed to everyone to see wild animals in their own haunts when they were not running nor hiding, nor looking about them in alarm. Yet Vassya saw foxes playing, hares washing themselves with their paws, bustards preening their wings and hammering out their hollow nests. Thanks to this keenness of sight, Vassya had, besides the world seen by everyone, another world of his own, accessible to no one else, and probably a very beautiful one, for when he saw something and was in raptures over it, it was impossible not to envy him.

When the waggons set off again, the church bells were ringing for service.

CHAPTER V

The train of waggons drew up on the bank of a river on one side of a village. The sun was blazing, as it had been the day before; the air was stagnant and depressing. There were a few willows on the bank, but the shade from them did not fall on the earth, but on the water, where it was wasted; even in the shade under the waggon it was stifling and wearisome. The water, blue from the reflection of the sky in it, was alluring.

Styopka, a waggoner whom Yegorushka noticed now for the first time, a Little Russian lad of eighteen, in a long shirt without a belt, and full trousers that flapped like flags as he walked, undressed quickly, ran along the steep bank and plunged into the water. He dived three times, then swam on his back and shut his eyes in his delight. His face was smiling and wrinkled up as though he were being tickled, hurt and amused.

On a hot day when there is nowhere to escape from the sultry, stifling heat, the splash of water and the loud breathing of a man bathing, sounds like good music to the ear. Dymov and Kiruha, looking at Styopka, undressed quickly and one after the other, laughing loudly in eager anticipation of their enjoyment, dropped into the water, and the quiet modest little river resounded with snorting and splashing and shouting. Kiruha coughed, laughed and shouted as though they were trying to drown him, while Dymov chased and tried to catch him by the leg.

'Ha-ha-ha!' he shouted. 'Catch him! Hold him!'

Kiruha laughed and enjoyed himself, but his expression was the same as it had been on dry land, stupid, with a look of astonishment on it as though someone had, unnoticed, stolen up behind him and hit him on the head with the butt-end of an axe. Yegorushka undressed, too, but did not let himself down by the bank, but took a run and a flying leap from the height of about ten feet. Describing an arc in the air, he fell into the water, sank deep, but did not reach the bottom; some force, cold and pleasant to the touch, seemed to hold him up and bring him back to the surface. He popped out and, snorting and blowing bubbles, opened his eyes; but the sun was reflected in the water quite close to his face. At first blinding spots of light, then rainbow colours and dark patches, flitted before his eyes. He made haste to dive again, opened his eyes in the water and saw something cloudy-green like a sky on a moonlight night. Again the same force would not let him touch the bottom and stay in the coolness, but lifted him to the surface. He popped out and heaved a sigh so deep that he had a feeling of space and freshness, not only in his chest, but in his stomach. Then, to get from the water everything he possibly could get, he allowed himself every luxury; he lay on his back and basked, splashed, frolicked, swam on his face, on his side, on his back and standing up – just as he pleased till he was exhausted. The other bank was thickly overgrown with reeds; it was golden in the sun, and the flowers of the reeds hung drooping to the water in lovely tassels. In one place the reeds were shaking and nodding, with their flowers rustling – Styopka and Kiruha were hunting crayfish.

'A crayfish, look, lads! A crayfish!' Kiruha cried triumphantly and actually showed a crayfish.

Yegorushka swam up to the reeds, dived, and began fumbling among their roots. Burrowing in the slimy, liquid mud, he felt something sharp and unpleasant – perhaps it really was a crayfish. But at that minute someone seized him by the leg and pulled him to the surface. Spluttering and coughing, Yegorushka opened his eyes and saw before him the wet grinning face of the dare-devil Dymov. The impudent fellow was breathing hard, and from a look in his eyes he seemed inclined for further mischief. He held Yegorushka tight by the leg, and was lifting his hand to take hold of his neck. But Yegorushka tore himself away with repulsion and terror, as though disgusted at being touched and afraid that the bully would drown him, and said:

'Fool! I'll punch you in the face.'

Feeling that this was not sufficient to express his hatred, he thought a minute and added:

'You blackguard! You son of a bitch!'

But Dymov, as though nothing were the matter, took no further notice of Yegorushka, but swam off to Kiruha, shouting:

'Ha-ha-ha! Let us catch fish! Mates, let us catch fish.'

'To be sure,' Kiruha agreed; 'there must be a lot of fish here.'

'Styopka, run to the village and ask the peasants for a net!'

'They won't give it to me.'

'They will, you ask them. Tell them that they should give it to us for Christ's sake, because we are just the same as pilgrims.'

'That's true.'

Styopka clambered out of the water, dressed quickly, and without a cap on he ran, his full trousers flapping, to the village. The water lost all its charm for Yegorushka after his encounter with Dymov. He got out and began dressing. Panteley and Vassya were sitting on the steep bank, with their legs hanging down, looking at the bathers. Emelyan was standing naked, up to his knees in the water, holding on to the grass with one hand to prevent himself from falling while the other stroked his body. With his bony shoulder-blades, with the swelling under his eye, bending down and evidently afraid of the water, he made a ludicrous figure. His face was grave and severe. He looked angrily at the water, as though he were just going to upbraid it for having given him cold in the Donets and robbed him of his voice.

'And why don't you bathe?' Yegorushka asked Vassya.

'Oh, I don't care for it. . . .' answered Vassya.

'How is it your chin is swollen?'

'It's bad. . . . I used to work at the match factory, little sir. . . . The doctor used to say that it would make my jaw rot. The air is not healthy there. There were three chaps beside me who had their jaws swollen, and with one of them it rotted away altogether.'

Styopka soon came back with the net. Dymov and Kiruha were already turning blue and getting hoarse by being so long in the water, but they set about fishing eagerly. First they went to a deep place beside the reeds; there Dymov was up to his neck, while the water went over squat Kiruha's head. The latter spluttered and blew bubbles, while Dymov stumbling on the prickly roots, fell over and got caught in the net; both flopped about in the water, and made a noise, and nothing but mischief came of their fishing.

'It's deep,' croaked Kiruha. 'You won't catch anything.'

'Don't tug, you devil!' shouted Dymov trying to put the net in the proper position. 'Hold it up.'

'You won't catch anything here,' Panteley shouted from the bank. 'You are only frightening the fish, you stupids! Go more to the left! It's shallower there!'

Once a big fish gleamed above the net; they all drew a breath, and Dymov struck the place where it had vanished with his fist, and his face expressed vexation.

'Ugh!' cried Panteley, and he stamped his foot. 'You've let the perch slip! It's gone!'

Moving more to the left, Dymov and Kiruha picked out a shallower place, and then fishing began in earnest. They had wandered off some hundred paces from the waggons; they could be seen silently trying to go as deep as they could and as near the reeds, moving their legs a little at a time, drawing out the nets, beating the water with their fists to drive them towards the nets. From the reeds they got to the further bank, they drew the net out, then, with a disappointed air, lifting their knees high as they walked, went back into the reeds. They were talking about something, but what it was no one could hear. The sun was scorching their backs, the flies were stinging them, and their bodies had turned from purple to crimson. Styopka was walking after them with a pail in his hands; he had tucked his shirt right up under his armpits, and was holding it up by the hem with his teeth. After every successful catch he lifted up some fish, and letting it shine in the sun, shouted:

'Look at this perch! We've five like that!'

Every time Dymov, Kiruha, and Styopka pulled out the net they could be seen fumbling about in the mud in it, putting some things into the pail and throwing other things away; sometimes they passed something that was in the net from hand to hand, examined it inquisitively, then threw that, too, away.

'What is it?' they shouted to them from the bank.

Styopka made some answer, but it was hard to make out his words. Then he climbed out of the water and, holding the pail in both hands, forgetting to let his shirt drop, ran to the waggons.

'It's full!' he shouted, breathing hard. 'Give us another!'

Yegorushka looked into the pail: it was full. A young pike poked its ugly nose out of the water, and there were swarms of crayfish and little fish round about it. Yegorushka put his hand down to the bottom and stirred up the water; the pike vanished under the crayfish, and a perch and a tench swam to the surface instead of it. Vassya, too, looked into the pail. His eyes grew moist and his face looked as caressing as before when he saw the fox. He took something out of the pail, put it to his mouth and began chewing it.

'Mates,' said Styopka in amazement, 'Vassya is eating a live gudgeon! Phoo!'

'It's not a gudgeon, but a minnow,' Vassya answered calmly, still munching.

He took a fish's tail out of his mouth, looked at it caressingly, and put it back again. While he was chewing and crunching with his teeth it seemed to Yegorushka that he saw before him something not human. Vassya's swollen chin, his lustreless eyes, his extraordinary sharp sight, the fish's tail in his mouth, and the caressing friendliness with which he crunched the gudgeon made him like an animal.

Yegorushka felt dreary beside him. And the fishing was over, too. He walked about beside the waggons, thought a little, and, feeling bored, strolled off to the village.

Not long afterwards he was standing in the church, and with his forehead leaning on somebody's back, listened to the singing of the choir. The service was drawing to a close. Yegorushka did not understand church singing and did not care for it. He listened a little, yawned, and began looking at the backs and heads before him. In one head, red and wet from his recent bathe, he recognized Emelyan. The back of his head had been cropped in a straight line higher than is usual; the hair in front had been cut unbecomingly high, and Emelyan's ears stood out like two dock leaves, and seemed to feel themselves out of place. Looking at the back of his head and his ears, Yegorushka, for some reason, thought that Emelyan was

probably very unhappy. He remembered the way he conducted with his hands, his husky voice, his timid air when he was
bathing, and felt intense pity for him. He longed to say
something friendly to him.

'I am here too,' he said, putting out his hand.

People who sing tenor or bass in the choir, especially those
who have at any time in their lives conducted, are accustomed
to look with a stern and unfriendly air at boys. They do not
give up this habit, even when they leave off being in a choir.
Turning to Yegorushka, Emelyan looked at him from under
his brows and said:

'Don't play in church!'

Then Yegorushka moved forwards nearer to the ikon-
stand. Here he saw interesting people. On the right side, in
front of everyone, a lady and a gentleman were standing on a
carpet. There were chairs behind them. The gentleman was
wearing newly ironed shantung trousers; he stood as
motionless as a soldier saluting, and held high his bluish
shaven chin. There was a very great air of dignity in his
stand-up collar, in his blue chin, in his small bald patch and his
cane. His neck was so strained from excess of dignity, and his
chin was drawn up so tensely, that it looked as though his
head were ready to fly off and soar upwards any minute. The
lady, who was stout and elderly and wore a white silk shawl,
held her head on one side and looked as though she had done
someone a favour, and wanted to say: "Oh, don't trouble
yourself to thank me; I don't like it. . . ." A thick wall of Little
Russian heads stood all round the carpet.

Yegorushka went up to the ikon-stand and began kissing
the local ikons. Before each image he slowly bowed down to
the ground, without getting up, looked round at the congreg-
ation, then got up and kissed the ikon. The contact of his
forehead with the cold floor afforded him great satisfaction.
When the beadle came from the altar with a pair of long
snuffers to put out the candles, Yegorushka jumped up
quickly from the floor and ran up to him.

'Have they given out the holy bread?' he asked.

'There is none, there is none,' the beadle muttered gruffly.
'It is no use your . . .'

The service was over; Yegorushka walked out of the

church in a leisurely way, and began strolling about the
market-place. He had seen a good many villages, market-
places, and peasants in his time, and everything that met his
eyes was entirely without interest for him. At a loss for
something to do, he went into a shop over the door of which
hung a wide strip of red cotton. The shop consisted of two
roomy, badly lighted parts; in one half they sold drapery and
groceries, in the other there were tubs of tar, and there were
horse-collars hanging from the ceiling; from both came the
unsavoury smell of leather and tar. The floor of the shop had
been watered; the man who watered it must have been a very
whimsical and original person, for it was sprinkled in
patterns and mysterious symbols. The shopkeeper, an
overfed-looking man with a broad face and round beard,
apparently a Great Russian, was standing, leaning his person
over the counter. He was nibbling a piece of sugar as he
drank his tea, and heaved a deep sigh at every sip. His face
expressed complete indifference, but each sigh seemed to be
saying:

'Just wait a minute; I will give it you.'

'Give me a farthing's worth of sunflower seeds,'
Yegorushka said, addressing him.

The shopkeeper raised his eyebrows, came out from
behind the counter, and poured a farthing's worth of
sunflower seeds into Yegorushka's pocket, using an empty
pomatum pot as a measure. Yegorushka did not want to go
away. He spent a long time in examining the box of cakes,
thought a little and asked, pointing to some little cakes
covered with the mildew of age:

'How much are these cakes?'

'Two for a farthing.'

Yegorushka took out of his pocket the cake given him the
day before by the Jewess, and asked him:

'And how much do you charge for cakes like this?'

The shopman took the cake in his hands, looked at it from
all sides, and raised one eyebrow.

'Like that?' he asked.

Then he raised the other eyebrow, thought a minute, and
answered:

'Two for three farthings. . . .'

A silence followed.

'Whose boy are you?' the shopman asked, pouring himself out some tea from a red copper teapot.

'The nephew of Ivan Ivanitch.'

'There are all sorts of Ivan Ivanitchs,' the shopkeeper sighed. He looked over Yegorushka's head towards the door, paused a minute and asked: 'Would you like some tea?'

'Please. . . .' Yegorushka assented not very readily, though he felt an intense longing for his usual morning tea.

The shopkeeper poured him out a glass and gave him with it a bit of sugar that looked as though it had been nibbled. Yegorushka sat down on the folding chair and began drinking it. He wanted to ask the price of a pound of sugar almonds, and had just broached the subject when a customer walked in, and the shopkeeper, leaving his glass of tea, attended to his business. He led the customer into the other half, where there was a smell of tar, and was there a long time discussing something with him. The customer, a man apparently very obstinate and pig-headed, was continually shaking his head to signify his disapproval, and retreating towards the door. The shopkeeper tried to persuade him of something and began pouring some oats into a big sack for him.

'Do you call those oats?' the customer said gloomily. 'Those are not oats, but chaff. It's a mockery to give that to the hens; enough to make the hens laugh. . . . No, I will go to Bondarenko.'

When Yegorushka went back to the river a small camp-fire was smoking on the bank. The waggoners were cooking their dinner. Styopka was standing in the smoke, stirring the cauldron with a big notched spoon. A little on one side Kiruha and Vassya, with eyes reddened from the smoke, were sitting cleaning the fish. Before them lay the net covered with slime and water weeds, and on it lay gleaming fish and crawling crayfish.

Emelyan, who had not long been back from the church, was sitting beside Panteley, waving his arm and humming just audibly in a husky voice: 'To Thee we sing. . . .' Dymov was moving about by the horses.

When they had finished cleaning them, Kiruha and Vassya

put the fish and the living crayfish together in the pail, rinsed them, and from the pail poured them all into the boiling water.

'Shall I put in some fat?' asked Styopka, skimming off the froth.

'No need. The fish will make its own gravy,' answered Kiruha.

Before taking the cauldron off the fire Styopka scattered into the water three big handfuls of millet and a spoonful of salt; finally he tried it, smacked his lips, licked the spoon, and gave a self-satisfied grunt, which meant that the grain was done.

All except Panteley sat down near the cauldron and set to work with their spoons.

'You there! Give the little lad a spoon!' Panteley observed sternly. 'I dare say he is hungry too!'

'Ours is peasant fare,' sighed Kiruha.

'Peasant fare is welcome, too, when one is hungry.'

They gave Yegorushka a spoon. He began eating, not sitting, but standing close to the cauldron and looking down into it as in a hole. The grain smelt of fish and fish-scales were mixed up with the millet. The crayfish could not be hooked out with a spoon, and the men simply picked them out of the cauldron with their hands; Vassya did so particularly freely, and wetted his sleeves as well as his hands in the mess. But yet the stew seemed to Yegorushka very nice, and reminded him of the crayfish soup which his mother used to make at home on fast-days. Panteley was sitting apart munching bread.

'Grandfather, why aren't you eating?' Emelyan asked him.

'I don't eat crayfish. . . . Nasty things,' the old man said, and turned away with disgust.

While they were eating they all talked. From this conversation Yegorushka gathered that all his new acquaintances, in spite of the differences of their ages and their characters, had one point in common which made them all alike: they were all people with a splendid past and a very poor present. Of their past they all – every one of them – spoke with enthusiasm; their attitude to the present was almost one of contempt. The Russian loves recalling life, but he does not love living. Yegorushka did not yet know that, and before the stew had been all eaten he firmly believed that the men sitting round the cauldron were the injured victims of fate. Panteley told them that in the past, before there were railways, he used to go with trains of waggons to Moscow and to Nizhni, and used to earn so much that he did not know what to do with his money; and what merchants there used to be in those days! what fish! how cheap everything was! Now the roads were shorter, the merchants were stingier, the peasants were poorer, the bread was dearer, everything had shrunk and was on a smaller scale. Emelyan told them that in old days he had been in the choir in Lugansky works, and that he had a remarkable voice and read music splendidly, while now he had become a peasant and lived on the charity of his brother, who sent him out with his horses and took half his earnings. Vassya had once worked in a match factory; Kiruha had been a coachman in a good family, and had been reckoned the smartest driver of a three-in-hand in the whole district. Dymov, the son of a well-to-do peasant, lived at ease, enjoyed himself and had known no trouble till he was twenty, when his stern harsh father, anxious to train him to work, and afraid he would be spoiled at home, had sent him to a carrier's to work as a hired labourer. Styopka was the only one who said nothing, but from his beardless face it was evident that his life had been a much better one in the past.

Thinking of his father, Dymov frowned and left off eating. Sullenly from under his brows he looked round at his companions and his eye rested upon Yegorushka.

'You heathen, take off your cap,' he said rudely. 'You can't eat with your cap on, and you a gentleman too!'

Yegorushka took off his hat and did not say a word, but the stew lost all savour for him, and he did not hear Panteley and Vassya intervening on his behalf. A feeling of anger with the insulting fellow was rankling oppressively in his breast, and he made up his mind that he would do him some injury, whatever it cost him.

After dinner everyone sauntered to the waggons and lay down in the shade.

'Are we going to start soon, grandfather?' Yegorushka asked Panteley.

'In God's good time we shall set off. . . . There's no starting yet; it is too hot. . . . O Lord, Thy will be done. Holy Mother. . . . Lie down, little lad.'

Soon there was a sound of snoring from under the waggons. Yegorushka meant to go back to the village, but on consideration, yawned and lay down by the old man.

CHAPTER VI

The waggons remained by the river the whole day, and set off again when the sun was setting.

Yegorushka was lying on the bales again; the waggon creaked softly and swayed from side to side. Panteley walked below, stamping his feet, slapping himself on his thighs and muttering. The air was full of the churring music of the steppes, as it had been the day before.

Yegorushka lay on his back, and, putting his hands under his head, gazed upwards at the sky. He watched the glow of sunset kindle, then fade away, guardian angels covering the horizon with their gold wings disposed themselves to slumber. The day had passed peacefully; the quiet peaceful night had come, and they could stay tranquilly at home in heaven. . . . Yegorushka saw the sky by degrees grow dark and the mist fall over the earth – saw the stars light up, one after the other. . . .

When you gaze a long while fixedly at the deep sky thoughts and feelings for some reason merge in a sense of loneliness. One begins to feel hopelessly solitary, and everything one used to look upon as near and akin becomes infinitely remote and valueless; the stars that have looked down from the sky thousands of years already, the mists and the incomprehensible sky itself, indifferent to the brief life of man, oppress the soul with their silence when one is left face to face with them and tries to grasp their significance. One is reminded of the solitude awaiting each one of us in the grave, and the reality of life seems awful . . . full of despair. . . .

Yegorushka thought of his grandmother, who was sleeping now under the cherry trees in the cemetery. He remembered how she lay in her coffin with pennies on her eyes, how afterwards she was shut in and let down into the grave; he even recalled the hollow sound of the clods of earth on the coffin lid. . . . He pictured his granny in the dark and narrow coffin, helpless and deserted by everyone. His imagination pictured his granny suddenly awakening, not understanding where she was, knocking upon the lid and calling for help, and in the end swooning with horror and dying again. He imagined his mother dead, Father Christopher, Countess Dranitzky, Solomon. But however much he tried to imagine himself in the dark tomb, far from home, outcast, helpless and dead, he could not succeed; for himself personally he could not admit the possibility of death, and felt that he would never die.

Panteley, for whom death could not be far away, walked below and went on reckoning up his thoughts.

'All right. . . . Nice gentlefolk. . . .' he muttered. 'Took his little lad to school – but how he is doing now I haven't heard say – in Slavyanoserbsk. I say there is no establishment for teaching them to be very clever. . . . No that's true – a nice little lad, no harm in him. . . . He'll grow up and be a help to his father. . . . You, Yegory, are little now, but you'll grow big and will keep your father and mother. . . . So it is ordained of God, "Honour your father and your mother". . . . I had children myself, but they were burnt. . . . My wife was burnt and my children. . . . that's true. . . . The hut caught fire on the night of Epiphany. . . . I was not at home, I was driving in Oryol. In Oryol. . . . Marya dashed out into the street, but remembering that the children were asleep in the hut, ran back and was burnt with her children. . . . Next day they found nothing but bones.'

About midnight Yegorushka and the waggoners were again sitting round a small camp fire. While the dry twigs and stems were burning up, Kiruha and Vassya went off somewhere to get water from a creek; they vanished into the darkness, but could be heard all the time talking and clinking their pails; so the creek was not far away. The light from the fire lay a great flickering patch on the earth; though the moon was bright, yet everything seemed impenitrably black beyond that red patch. The light was in the waggoners' eyes, and they saw only part of the great road; almost unseen in the darkness the waggons with the bales and the horses looked like a mountain of undefined shape. Twenty paces from the camp fire at the edge of the road stood a wooden cross that had fallen aslant. Before the camp fire had been lighted, when he could still see things at a distance, Yegorushka had noticed that there was a similar old slanting cross on the other side of the great road.

Coming back with the water, Kiruha and Vassya filled the cauldron and fixed it over the fire. Styopka, with the notched spoon in his hand, took his place in the smoke by the cauldron, gazing dreamily into the water for the scum to rise. Panteley and Emelyan were sitting side by side in silence, brooding over something. Dymov was lying on his stomach, with his head propped on his fists, looking into the fire. . . . Styopka's shadow was dancing over him, so that his handsome face was at one minute covered with darkness, at the next lighted up. . . . Kiruha and Vassya were wandering about at a little distance gathering dry grass and bark for the fire. Yegorushka, with his hands in his pockets, was standing by Panteley, watching how the fire devoured the grass.

All were resting, musing on something, and they glanced cursorily at the cross over which patches of red light were dancing. There is something melancholy, pensive, and extremely poetical about a solitary tomb; one feels its silence, and the silence gives one the sense of the presence of the soul of the unknown man who lies under the cross. Is that soul at peace on the steppe? Does it grieve in the moonlight? Near the tomb the steppe seems melancholy, dreary and mournful; the grass seems more sorrowful, and one fancies the grasshoppers chirrup less freely, and there is no passer-by who would not remember that lonely soul and keep looking back at the tomb, till it was left far behind and hidden in the mists. . . .

'Grandfather, what is that cross for?' asked Yegorushka.

Panteley looked at the cross and then at Dymov and asked:

'Nikola, isn't this the place where the mowers killed the merchants?'

Dymov not very readily raised himself on his elbow, looked at the road and said:

'Yes, it is. . . .'

A silence followed. Kiruha broke up some dry stalks, crushed them up together and thrust them under the cauldron. The fire flared up brightly; Styopka was enveloped in black smoke, and the shadow cast by the cross danced along the road in the dusk beside the waggons.

'Yes, they were killed,' Dymov said reluctantly. 'Two merchants, father and son, were travelling, selling holy images. They put up in the inn not far from here that is now kept by Ignat Fomin. The old man had a drop too much, and began boasting that he had a lot of money with him. We all know merchants are a boastful set, God preserve us. . . . They can't resist showing off before the likes of us. And at the time some mowers were staying the night at the inn. So they overheard what the merchants said and took note of it.'

'Oh Lord! . . . Holy Mother!' sighed Panteley.

'Next day, as soon as it was light,' Dymov went on, 'the merchants were preparing to set off and the mowers tried to join them. "Let us go together, your worship. It will be more cheerful and there will be less danger, for this is an out-of-the-way place. . . ." The merchants had to travel at a walking pace to avoid breaking the images, and that just suited the mowers. . . .'

Dymov rose into a kneeling position and stretched.

'Yes,' he went on, yawning. 'Everything went all right till they reached this spot, and then the mowers let fly at them with their scythes. The son, he was a fine young fellow, snatched the scythe from one of them, and he used it too. . . . Well, of course, they got the best of it because there were eight of them. They hacked at the merchants so that there was not a sound place left on their bodies: when they had finished they dragged both of them off the road, the father to one side and the son to the other. Opposite that cross there is another cross on this side. . . . Whether it is still standing, I don't know. . . . I can't see it from here. . . .'

'It is,' said Kiruha.

'They say they did not find much money afterwards.'

'No,' Panteley confirmed; 'they only found a hundred roubles.'

'And three of them died afterwards, for the merchant had cut them badly with the scythe, too. They died from loss of blood. One had his hand cut off, so that they say he ran three miles without his hand, and they found him on a mound close to Kurikovo. He was squatting on his heels, with his head on his knees, as though he were lost in thought, but when they looked at him there was no life in him and he was dead. . . .'

'They found him by the track of blood,' said Panteley.

Everyone looked at the cross, and again there was a hush. From somewhere, most likely from the creek, floated the mournful cry of the bird: 'Sleep! sleep! sleep!'

'There are a great many wicked people in the world,' said Emelyan.

'A great many,' assented Panteley, and he moved up closer to the fire as though he were frightened. 'A great many,' he went on in a low voice. 'I've seen lots and lots of them. . . . Wicked people! . . . I have seen a great many holy and just, too. . . . Queen of Heaven, save us and have mercy on us. I remember once thirty years ago, or maybe more, I was driving a merchant from Morshansk. The merchant was a jolly handsome fellow, with money, too . . , the merchant was . . . a nice man, no harm in him. . . So we put him up for the night at an inn. And in Russia the inns are not what they are in these parts. There the yards are roofed in and look like the ground floor, or let us say like barns in good farms. Only a barn would be a bit higher. So we put up there and were all right. My merchant was in a room, while I was with the horses, and everything was as it should be. So, lads, I said my prayers before going to sleep and began walking about the yard. And it was a dark night, I couldn't see anything; it was no good trying. So I walked about a bit up to the waggons, or nearly, when I saw a light gleaming. What could it mean? I thought the people of the inn had gone to bed long ago, and besides the merchant and me there were no other guests in the inn. . . Where could the light have come from? I felt suspicious. . . . I went closer . . . towards the light. . . . The Lord have mercy upon me! and save me, Queen of Heaven! I looked and there was a little window with a grating. . . . close to the ground, in the house. . . . I lay down on the ground and looked in; as soon as I looked in a cold chill ran all down me. . . .'

Kiruha, trying not to make a noise, thrust a handful of twigs into the fire. After waiting for it to leave off crackling and hissing, the old man went on:

'I looked in and there was a big cellar, black and dark. . . . There was a lighted lantern on a tub. In the middle of the cellar were about a dozen men in red shirts with their sleeves turned up, sharpening long knives. . . . Ugh! So we had fallen into a nest of robbers. . . .What's to be done? I ran to the merchant, woke him up quietly, and said: "Don't be frightened, merchant", said I, "but we are in a bad way. We have fallen into a nest of robbers", I said. He turned pale and asked: "What are we to do now, Panteley? I have a lot of money that belongs to orphans. As for my life", he said, "that's in God's hands. I am not afraid to die, but it's dreadful to lose the orphans' money", said he. . . . What were we to do? The gates were locked; there was no getting out. If there had been a fence one could have climbed over it, but with the yard shut up! . . . "Come, don't be frightened, merchant", said I; "but pray to God. Maybe the Lord will not let the orphans suffer. Stay still", said I, "and make no sign, and meanwhile, maybe, I shall think of something. . . ." Right! . . . I prayed to God and the Lord put the thought into my mind. . . . I clambered up on my chaise and softly. . . . softly so that no one should hear, began pulling out the straw in the thatch, made a hole and crept out, crept out. . . . Then I jumped off the roof and ran along the road as fast as I could. I ran and ran till I was nearly dead. . . . I ran maybe four miles without taking breath, if not more. Thank God I saw a village. I ran up to a hut and began tapping at a window. "Good Christian people," I said, and told them all about it, "do not let a Christian soul perish." I waked them all up. . . . The peasants gathered together and went with me. . . . one with a cord, one with an oakstick, others with pitchforks. . . . We broke in the gates of the innyard and went straight to the cellar. . . . And the robbers had just finished sharpening their knives and were going to kill the merchant. The peasants took them, every one of them, bound them and carried them to the police. The merchant gave them three hundred roubles in his joy, and gave me five gold pieces and put my name down. They said that they found human bones in the cellar afterwards, heaps and heaps of them. . . . Bones! . . . So they robbed people and then buried them, so that there should be no traces. . . . Well, afterwards they were punished at Morshansk.'

Panteley had finished his story, and he looked round at his listeners. They were gazing at him in silence. The water was boiling by now and Styopka was skimming off the froth.

'Is the fat ready?' Kiruha asked him in a whisper.

'Wait a little. . . . Directly.'

Styopka, his eyes fixed on Panteley as though he were afraid that the latter might begin some story before he was back, ran to the waggons; soon he came back with a little wooden bowl and began pounding some lard in it.

'I went another journey with a merchant, too. . . .' Panteley went on again, speaking as before in a low voice and with fixed unblinking eyes. 'His name, as I remember now, was Pyotr Grigoritch. He was a nice man. . . . the merchant was. We stopped in the same way at an inn. . . . He indoors and me with the horses. . . . The people of the house, the innkeeper and his wife, seemed friendly good sort of people; the labourers, too, seemed all right; but yet, lads, I couldn't sleep. I had a queer feeling in my heart. . . . a queer feeling, that was just it. The gates were open and there were plenty of people about, and yet I felt afraid and not of myself. Everyone had been asleep long ago. It was the middle of the night; it would soon be time to get up, and I was lying alone in my chaise and could not close my eyes, as though I were some owl. And then, lads, I heard this sound, "Toop! toop! toop!" Someone was creeping up to the chaise. I poke my head out, and there was a peasant woman in nothing but her shift and with her feet bare. . . . "What do you want, good woman?" I asked. And she was all of a tremble; her face was terror-stricken. . . . "Get up, good man," said she; "the people are plotting evil. . . . They mean to kill your merchant. With my own ears I heard the master whispering with his wife. . . ." So it was not for nothing the foreboding of my heart! "And who are you?" I asked. "I am their cook," she said. . . . Right! . . . So I got out of the chaise and went to the merchant. I waked him up and said: "Things aren't quite right, Pyotr Grigoritch. . . . Make haste and rouse yourself from sleep, your worship, and dress now while there is still time", I said; "and to save our skins, let us get away from trouble". He had no sooner begun dressing when the door opened and, mercy on us! I saw, Holy Mother! the innkeeper and his wife come into the room with three labourers. So they had persuaded the labourers to join them. "The merchant has a lot of money, and we'll go shares", they told them. Every one of the five had a

long knife in their hand . . . each a knife. The innkeeper
locked the door and said: "Say your prayers, travellers. . . .
and if you begin screaming," they said, "we won't let you say
your prayers before you die. . . ." As though we could
scream! I had such a lump in my throat I could not cry
out. . . . The merchant wept and said: "Good Christian
people! you have resolved to kill me because my money
tempts you. Well, so be it; I shall not be the first nor shall I be
the last. Many of us merchants have been murdered at inns.
But why, good Christian brothers," says he, "murder my
driver? Why should he have to suffer for my money?" And he
said that so pitifully! And the innkeeper answered him: "If we
leave him alive", said he, "he will be the first to bear witness
against us. One may just as well kill two as one. You can but
answer once for seven misdeeds. . . . Say your prayers, that's
all you can do, and it is no good talking!" The merchant and I
knelt down side by side and wept and said our prayers. He
thought of his children. I was young in those days; I wanted to
live. . . . We looked at the images and prayed, and so pitifully
that it brings a tear even now. . . . And the innkeeper's wife
looks at us and says: "Good people," said she, "don't bear a
grudge against us in the other world and pray to God for our
punishment, for it is want that drives us to it". We prayed and
wept and prayed and wept, and God heard us. He had pity on
us, I suppose. . . . At the very minute when the innkeeper had
taken the merchant by the beard to rip open his throat with his
knife suddenly someone seemed to tap at the window from
the yard! We all started, and the innkeeper's hands dropped. . . .Someone was tapping at the window and shouting:
"Pyotr Grigoritch," he shouted, "are you here? Get ready and
let's go!" The people saw that someone had come for the
merchant; they were terrified and took to their heels. . . . And
we made haste into the yard, harnessed the horses, and were
out of sight in a minute. . . .'

'Who was it knocked at the window?' asked Dymov.

'At the window? It must have been a holy saint or angel, for
there was no one else. . . . When we drove out of the yard
there wasn't a soul in the street. . . . It was the Lord's doing.'

Panteley told other stories, and in all of them "long knives"
figured and all alike sounded made up. Had he heard these

stories from someone else, or had he made them up himself in the remote past, and afterwards, as his memory grew weaker, mixed up his experiences with his imaginations and become unable to distinguish one from another? Anything is possible, but it is strange that on this occasion and for the rest of the journey, whenever he happened to tell a story, he gave unmistakable preference to fiction, and never told of what he really had experienced. At the time Yegorushka took it all for the genuine thing, and believed every word; later on it seemed to him strange that a man who in his day had travelled all over Russia and seen and known so much, whose wife and children had been burnt to death, so failed to appreciate the wealth of his life that whenever he was sitting by the camp fire he was either silent or talked of what had never been.

Over their porridge they were all silent, thinking of what they had just heard. Life is terrible and marvellous, and so, however terrible a story you tell in Russia, however you embroider it with nests of robbers, long knives and such marvels, it always finds an echo of reality in the soul of the listener, and only a man who has been a good deal affected by education looks askance distrustfully, and even he will be silent. The cross by the roadside, the dark bales of wool, the wide expanse of the plain, and the lot of the men gathered together by the camp fire – all this was of itself so marvellous and terrible that the fantastic colours of legend and fairy-tale were pale and blended with life.

All the others ate out of the cauldron, but Panteley sat apart and ate his porridge out of a wooden bowl. His spoon was not like those the others had, but was made of cypress wood, with a little cross on it. Yegorushka, looking at him, thought of the little ikon glass and asked Styopka softly:

'Why does Grandfather sit apart?'

'He is an Old Believer,' Styopka and Vassya answered in a whisper. And as they said it they looked as though they were speaking of some secret vice or weakness.

All sat silent, thinking. After the terrible stories there was no inclination to speak of ordinary things. All at once in the midst of the silence Vassya drew himself up and, fixing his lustreless eyes on one point, pricked up his ears.

'What is it?' Dymov asked him.

'Someone is coming,' answered Vassya.

'Where do you see him?'

'Yo-on-der! There's something white. . . .'

There was nothing to be seen but darkness in the direction in which Vassya was looking; everyone listened, but they could hear no sound of steps.

'Is he coming by the highroad?' asked Dymov.

'No, over the open country. . . . He is coming this way.'

A minute passed in silence.

'And maybe it's the merchant who was buried here walking over the steppe,' said Dymov.

All looked askance at the cross, exchanged glances and suddenly broke into a laugh. They felt ashamed of their terror.

'Why should he walk?' asked Panteley. 'It's only those walk at night whom the earth will not take to herself. And the merchants were all right. . . . The merchants have received the crown of martyrs.'

But all at once they heard the sound of steps; someone was coming in haste.

'He's carrying something,' said Vassya.

They could hear the grass rustling and the dry twigs crackling under the feet of the approaching wayfarer. But from the glare of the camp fire nothing could be seen. At last the steps sounded close by, and someone coughed. The flickering light seemed to part; a veil dropped from the waggoner's eyes, and they saw a man facing them.

Whether it was due to the flickering light or because everyone wanted to make out the man's face first of all, it happened, strangely enough, that at the first glance at him they all saw, first of all, not his face nor his clothes, but his smile. It was an extraordinarily good-natured, broad, soft smile, like that of a baby on waking, one of those infectious smiles to which it is difficult not to respond by smiling too. The stranger, when they did get a good look at him, turned out to be a man of thirty, ugly and in no way remarkable. He was a tall Little Russian, with a long nose, long arms and long legs; everything about him seemed long except his neck, which was so short that it made him seem stooping. He was wearing a clean white shirt with an embroidered collar, white trousers, and new high boots, and in comparison with the waggoners he looked quite a dandy. In his arms he was carrying something big, white, and at the first glance strange-looking, and the stock of a gun also peeped out from behind his shoulder.

Coming from the darkness into the circle of light, he stopped short as though petrified, and for half a minute looked at the waggoners as though he would have said: 'Just look what a smile I have!'

Then he took a step towards the fire, smiled still more radiantly and said:

'Bread and salt, friends!'

'You are very welcome!' Panteley answered for them all.

The stranger put down by the fire what he was carrying in his arms – it was a dead buzzard – and greeted them once more.

They all went up to the buzzard and began examining it.

'A fine big bird; what did you kill it with?' asked Dymov.

'Grape-shot. You can't get him with small shot; he won't let you get near enough. Buy it, friends! I will let you have it for twenty kopecks.'

'What use would it be to us? It's good roast, but I bet it would be tough boiled; you could not get your teeth into it. . .'

'Oh, what a pity! I would take it to the gentry at the farm; they would give me half a rouble for it. But it's a long way to go – twelve miles!'

The stranger sat down, took off his gun and laid it beside him.

He seemed sleepy and languid; he sat smiling, and, screwing up his eyes at the firelight, apparently thinking of something very agreeable. They gave him a spoon; he began eating.

'Who are you?' Dymov asked him.

The stranger did not hear the question; he made no answer, and did not even glance at Dymov. Most likely this smiling man did not taste the flavour of the porridge either, for he seemed to eat it mechanically, lifting the spoon to his lips sometimes very full and sometimes quite empty. He was not drunk, but he seemed to have something nonsensical in his head.

'I ask you who you are' repeated Dymov.

'I?' said the unknown, starting. 'Konstantin Zvonik from Rovno. It's three miles from here.'

And anxious to show straight off that he was not quite an ordinary peasant, but something better, Konstantin hastened to add:

'We keep bees and fatten pigs.'

'Do you live with your father or in a house of your own?'

'No; now I am living in a house of my own. I have parted. This month, just after St. Peter's Day, I got married. I am a married man now! . . . . It's eighteen days since the wedding.'

'That's a good thing,' said Panteley. 'Marriage is a good thing. . . . God's blessing on it.'

'His young wife sits at home while he rambles about the steppe,' laughed Kiruha. 'Queer chap!'

As though he had been pinched on the tenderest spot, Konstantin started, laughed and flushed crimson.

'But, Lord, she is not at home!' he said quickly, taking the spoon out of his mouth and looking round at everyone with an expression of delight and wonder. 'She is not; she has gone to her mother's for three days! Yes, indeed, she has gone away, and I feel as though I were not married. . . .'

Konstantin waved his hand and turned his head; he wanted to go on thinking, but the joy which beamed in his face prevented him. As though he were not comfortable, he changed his attitude, laughed, and again waved his hand. He was ashamed to share his happy thoughts with strangers, but at the same time he had an irresistible longing to communicate his joy.

'She has gone to Demidovo to see her mother,' he said, blushing and moving his gun. 'She'll be back tomorrow. . . . She said she would be back to dinner.'

'And you miss her?' said Dymov.

'Oh, Lord, yes; I should think so. We have only been married such a little while, and she has gone away. . . . Eh! Oh, but she is a tricksy one, God strike me dead! She is such a fine, splendid girl, such a one for laughing and singing, full of life and fire! When she is there your brain is in a whirl, and now she is away I wander about the steppe like a fool, as though I had lost something. I have been walking since dinner.'

Konstantin rubbed his eyes, looked at the fire and laughed.

'You love her, then. . . .' said Panteley.

'She is so fine and splendid,' Konstantin repeated, not hearing him; 'such a housewife, clever and sensible. You wouldn't find another like her among simple folk in the whole province. She has gone away. . . . But she is missing me, I kno–ow! I know the little magpie. She said she would be back tomorrow by dinner-time. . . . And just think how queer!' Konstantin almost shouted, speaking a note higher and shifting his position. 'Now she loves me and is sad without me, and yet she would not marry me.'

'But eat,' said Kiruha.

'She would not marry me,' Konstantin went on, not heeding him. 'I have been struggling with her for three years! I saw her at the Kalatchik fair; I fell madly in love with her, was ready to hang myself. . . . I live at Rovno, she at Demidovo, more than twenty miles apart, and there was nothing I could do. I sent match-makers to her, and all she said was: "I won't!" Ah, the magpie! I sent her one thing and another, earrings and cakes, and twenty pounds of honey – but still she said "I won't!" And there it was. If you come to think of it, I was not a match for her! She was young and lovely, full of fire, while I am old: I shall soon be thirty, and a regular beauty, too; a fine beard like a goat's, a clear complexion all covered with pimples – how could I be compared with her! The only thing to be said is that we are well off, but then the Vahramenkys are well off, too. They've six oxen, and they keep a couple of labourers. I was in love, friends, as though I were plague-stricken. I couldn't sleep or eat; my brain was full of thoughts, and in such a maze, Lord preserve us! I longed to see her, and she was in Demidovo. What do you think? God be my witness, I am not lying, three times a week I walked over there on foot just to have a look at her. I gave up my work! I was so frantic that I even wanted to get taken on as a labourer in Demidovo, so as to be near her. I was in misery! My mother called in a witch a dozen times; my father tried thrashing me. For three years I was in this torment, and then I made up my mind. "Damn my soul!" I said, "I will go to the town and be a cabman. . . . It seems it is fated not to be". At Easter I went to Demidovo to have a last look at her. . . .'

Konstantin threw back his head and went off into a mirthful tinkling laugh, as though had just taken someone in very cleverly.

'I saw her by the river with the lads,' he went on. 'I was overcome with anger. . . . I called her aside and maybe for a full hour I said all manner of things to her. She fell in love with me! For three years she did not like me! she fell in love with me for what I said to her. . . .'

'What did you say to her?' asked Dymov.

'What did I say? I don't remember. . . . How could one remember? My words flowed at the time like water from a tap, without stopping to take breath. Ta-ta-ta! And now I can't utter a word. . . . Well, so she married me. . . . She's gone now to her mother's, the magpie, and while she is away here I wander over the steppe. I can't stay at home. It's more than I can do!'

Konstantin awkwardly released his feet, on which he was siting, stretched himself on the earth, and propped his head in his fists, then got up and sat down again. Everyone by now thoroughly understood that he was in love and happy, poignantly happy; his smile, his eyes, and every movement, expressed fervent happiness. He could not find a place for himself, and did not know what attitude to take to keep himself from being overwhelmed by the multitude of his delightful thoughts. Having poured out his soul before these strangers, he settled down quietly at last, and, looking at the fire, sank into thought.

At the sight of this happy man everyone felt depressed and longed to be happy, too. Everyone was dreamy. Dymov got up, walked about softly by the fire, and from his walk, from the movement of his shoulder-blades, it could be seen that he was weighed down by depression and yearning. He stood still for a moment, looked at Konstantin and sat down.

The camp fire had died down by now; there was no flicker, and the patch of red had grown small and dim. . . . And as the fire went out the moonlight grew clearer and clearer. Now they could see the full width of the road, the bales of wool, the shafts of the waggons, the munching horses; on the further side of the road there was the dim outline of the second cross. . . .

Dymov leaned his cheek on his hand and softly hummed some plaintive song. Konstantin smiled drowsily and chimed in with a thin voice. They sang for half a minute, then sank into silence. Emelyan started, jerked his elbows and wriggled his fingers.

'Lads,' he said in an imploring voice, 'let's sing something sacred!' Tears came into his eyes. 'Lads,' he repeated, pressing his hands on his heart, 'let's sing something sacred!'

'I don't know anything,' said Konstantin.

Everyone refused, then Emelyan sang alone. He waved both arms, nodded his head, opened his mouth, but nothing came from his throat but a discordant gasp. He sang with his arms, with his head, with his eyes, even with the swelling on his face; he sang passionately with anguish, and the more he strained his chest to extract at least one note from it, the more discordant were his gasps. . . .

Yegorushka, like the rest, was overcome with depression. He went to his waggon, clambered up on the bales, and lay down. He looked at the sky, and thought of happy Konstantin and his wife. Why did people get married? What were women in the world for? Yegorushka put the vague questions to himself, and thought that a man would certainly be happy if he had an affectionate, merry and beautiful woman continually living at his side. For some reason he remembered the Countess Dranitsky, and thought it would probably be very pleasant to live with a woman like that; he would perhaps have married her with pleasure if that idea had not been so shameful. He recalled her eyebrows, the pupils of her eyes, her carriage, the clock with the horseman. . . . The soft warm night moved softly down upon him and whispered something in his ear, and it seemed to him that it was that lovely woman bending over him, looking at him with a smile and meaning to kiss him. . . .

Nothing was left of the fire but two little red eyes, which kept on growing smaller and smaller. Konstantin and the waggoners were sitting by it, dark motionless figures, and it seemed as though there were many more of them than before. The twin crosses were equally visible, and far, far away, somewhere by the highroad there gleamed a red light – other people cooking their porridge, most likely.

'Our Mother Russia is the he-ad of all the world!' Kiruha sang out suddenly in a harsh voice, choked and subsided. The steppe echo caught up his voice, carried it on, and it seemed as though stupidity itself were rolling on heavy wheels over the steppe.

'It's time to go,' said Panteley. 'Get up, lads.'

While they were putting the horses in, Konstantin walked by the waggons and talked rapturously of his wife.

'Good-bye, mates!' he cried when the waggons started. 'Thank you for your hospitality. I shall go on again towards that light. It's more than I can stand.'

And he quickly vanished in the mist, and for a long time they could hear him striding in the direction of the light to tell those other strangers of his happiness.

When Yegorushka woke up next day it was early morning; the sun had not yet risen. The waggons were at a standstill. A man in a white cap and a suit of cheap grey material, mounted on a little Cossack stallion, was talking to Dymov and Kiruha beside the foremost waggon. A mile and a half ahead there were long low white barns and little houses with tiled roofs; there were neither yards nor trees to be seen beside the little houses.

'What village is that, Grandfather?' asked Yegorushka.

'That's the Armenian Settlement, youngster,' answered Panteley. 'The Armenians live there. They are a good sort of people. . . . the Armenians are.'

The man in grey had finished talking to Dymov and Kiruha; he pulled up his little stallion and looked across towards the settlement.

'What a business, only think!' sighed Panteley, looking towards the settlement, too, and shuddering at the morning freshness. 'He has sent a man to the settlement for some papers, and he doesn't come. . . . He should have sent Styopka.'

'Who is that, Grandfather?' asked Yegorushka.

'Varlamov.'

My goodness! Yegorushka jumped up quickly, getting upon his knees, and looked at the white cap. It was hard to recognize the mysterious elusive Varlamov, who was sought by every-one, who was always 'on his rounds,' and who had far more money than Countess Dranitzky, in the short, grey little man in big boots, who was sitting on an ugly little nag and talking to peasants at an hour when all decent people were asleep.

'He is all right, a good man,' said Panteley, looking towards
the settlement. 'God give him health – a splendid gentleman,
Semyon Alexandritch. . . . It's people like that the earth rests
upon. That's true. . . . The cocks are not crowing yet, and he
is already up and about. . . . Another man would be asleep, or
gallivanting with visitors at home, but he is on the steppe all
day. . . . on his rounds. . . . He does not let things slip. . . .
No-o! He's a fine fellow. . . .'

Varlamov was talking about something, while he kept his
eyes fixed. The little stallion shifted from one leg to another
impatiently.

'Semyon Alexandritch!' cried Panteley, taking off his hat.
'Allow us to send Styopka! Emelyan, call out that Styopka
should be sent.'

But now at last a man on horseback could be seen coming
from the settlement. Bending very much to one side and
brandishing his whip above his head like a gallant young
Caucasian, and wanting to astonish everyone by his
horsemanship, he flew towards the waggons with the
swiftness of a bird.

'That must be one of his circuit men,' said Panteley. 'He
must have a hundred such horsemen or maybe more.'

Reaching the first waggon, he pulled up his horse, and
taking off his hat, handed Varlamov a little book. Varlamov
took several papers out of the book, read them and cried:

'And where is Ivantchuk's letter?'

The horseman took the book back, looked at the papers and
shrugged his shoulders. He began saying something, probably
justifying himself and asking to be allowed to ride back to the
settlement again. The little stallion suddenly stirred as though
Varlamov had grown heavier. Varlamov stirred too.

'Go along!' he cried angrily, and he waved his whip at the
man.

Then he turned his horse round and, looking through the
papers in the book, moved at a walking pace alongside the
waggons. When he reached the hindmost, Yegorushka
strained his eyes to get a better look at him. Varlamov was an
elderly man. His face, a simple Russian sunburnt face with a
small grey beard, was red, wet with dew and covered with
little blue veins; it had the same expression of businesslike

coldness as Ivan Ivanitch's face, the same look of fanatical zeal for business. But yet what a difference could be felt between him and Kuzmitchov! Uncle Ivan Ivanitch always had on his face, together with his businesslike reserve, a look of anxiety and apprehension that he would not find Varlamov, that he would be late, that he would miss a good price; nothing of that sort, so characteristic of small and dependent persons, could be seen in the face or figure of Varlamov. This man made the price himself, was not looking for anyone, and did not depend on anyone; however ordinary his exterior, yet in everything, even in the manner of holding his whip, there was a sense of power and habitual authority over the steppe.

As he rode by Yegorushka he did not glance at him. Only the little stallion deigned to notice Yegorushka; he looked at him with his large foolish eyes, and even he showed no interest. Panteley bowed to Varlamov; the latter noticed it, and without taking his eyes off the sheets of paper, said lisping:

'How are you, old man?'

Varlamov's conversation with the horseman and the way he had brandished his whip had evidently made an overwhelming impression on the whole party. Everyone looked grave. The man on horseback, cast down at the anger of the great man, remained stationary, with his hat off, and the rein loose by the foremost waggon; he was silent, and seemed unable to grasp that the day had begun so badly for him.

'He is a harsh old man. . . .' muttered Panteley. 'It's a pity he is so harsh! But he is all right, a good man. . . . He doesn't abuse men for nothing. . . . It's no matter. . . .'

After examining the papers, Varlamov thrust the book into his pocket; the little stallion, as though he knew what was in his mind, without waiting for orders, started and dashed along the highroad.

CHAPTER VII

On the following night the waggoners had halted and were cooking their porridge. On this occasion there was a sense of overwhelming oppression over everyone. It was sultry; they all drank a great deal, but could not quench their thirst. The moon was intensely crimson and sullen, as though it were sick. The stars, too, were sullen, the mist was thicker, the distance more clouded. Nature seemed as though languid and weighed down by some foreboding.

There was not the same liveliness and talk round the camp fire as there had been the day before. All were dreary and spoke listlessly and without interest. Panteley did nothing but sigh and complain of his feet, and continually alluded to impenitent deathbeds.

Dymov was lying on his stomach, chewing a straw in silence; there was an expression of disgust on his face as though the straw smelt unpleasant, a spiteful and exhausted look. . . . Vassya complained that his jaw ached, and prophesied bad weather; Emelyan was not waving his arms, but sitting still and looking gloomily at the fire. Yegorushka, too, was weary. This slow travelling exhausted him, and the sultriness of the day had given him a headache.

While they were cooking the porridge, Dymov, to relieve his boredom, began quarrelling with his companions.

'Here he lolls, the lumpy face, and is the first to put his spoon in,' he said, looking spitefully at Emelyan. 'Greedy! always contrives to sit next the cauldron. He's been a church-singer, so he thinks he is a gentleman! There are a lot of singers like you begging along the highroad!'

'What are you pestering me for?' asked Emelyan, looking at him angrily.

'To teach you not to be the first to dip into the cauldron. Don't think too much of yourself!'

'You are a fool, and that is all about it!' wheezed out Emelyan.

Knowing by experience how such conversations usually ended, Panteley and Vassya intervened and tried to persuade Dymov not to quarrel about nothing.

'A church-singer!' The bully would not desist, but laughed contemptuously. 'Anyone can sing like that – sit in the church porch and sing "Give me alms, for Christ's sake!" Ugh! you are a nice fellow!'

Emelyan did not speak. His silence had an irritating effect on Dymov. He looked with still greater hatred at the ex-singer and said:

'I don't care to have anything to do with you, or I would show you what to think of yourself.'

'But why are you pushing me, you Mazeppa?' Emelyan cried, flaring up. 'Am I interfering with you?'

'What did you call me?' asked Dymov, drawing himself up, and his eyes were suffused with blood. 'Eh! I am a Mazeppa? Yes? Take that, then; go and look for it.'

Dymov snatched the spoon out of Emelyan's hand and flung it far away. Kiruha, Vassya, and Styopka ran to look for it, while Emelyan fixed an imploring and questioning look on Panteley. His face suddenly became small and wrinkled; it began twitching, and the ex-singer began to cry like a child.

Yegorushka, who had long hated Dymov, felt as though the air all at once were unbearably stifling, as though the fire were scorching his face; he longed to run quickly to the waggons in the darkness, but the bully's angry, bored eyes drew the boy to him. With a passionate desire to say something extremely offensive, he took a step towards Dymov, and brought out, gasping for breath:

'You are the worst of the lot; I can't bear you!'

After this he ought to have run to the waggons, but he could not stir from the spot, and went on:

'In the next world you will burn in hell! I'll complain to Ivan Ivanitch. Don't you dare insult Emelyan!'

'Say this too, please,' laughed Dymov: '"every little sucking-pig wants to lay down the law." Shall I pull your ear?'

Yegorushka felt that he could not breathe; and something which had never happened to him before – he suddenly began shaking all over, stamping his feet and crying shrilly:

'Beat him, beat him!'

Tears gushed from his eyes: he felt ashamed, and ran staggering back to the waggon. The effect produced by this outburst he did not see. Lying on the bales and twitching his arms and legs, he whispered:

'Mother, mother!'

And these men and the shadows round the camp fire, and the dark bales and the far away lightning, which was flashing every minute in the distance – all struck him now as terrible and unfriendly. He was overcome with terror, and asked himself in despair why and how he had come into this unknown land in the company of terrible peasants? Where was his uncle now, where was Father Christopher, where was Deniska? Why were they so long in coming? Had they forgotten him? At the thought that he was forgotten and cast out to the mercy of fate, he felt such a cold chill of dread that he had several times an impulse to jump off the bales of wool and run back full speed along the road; but the thought of the huge dark crosses, which would certainly meet him on the way, and the lightning flashing in the distance, stopped him. . . . And only when he whispered, 'Mother, mother!' he felt as it were a little better.

The waggoners must have been full of dread, too. After Yegorushka had run away from the camp fire they sat at first for a long time in silence, then they began speaking in hollow undertones about something, saying that it was coming and that they must make haste and get away from it. . . . They quickly finished supper, put out the fire and began harnessing the horses in silence. From their fluster and the broken phrases they uttered it was apparent they saw some trouble. Before they set off on their way, Dymov went up to Panteley and asked softly:

'What's his name?'

'Yegory,' answered Panteley.

Dymov put one foot on the wheel, caught hold of the cord which was tied round the bales, and pulled himself up. Yegorushka saw his face and curly head. The face was pale and looked grave and exhausted, but there was no expression of spite in it.

'Yera!' he said softly, 'here, hit me!'

Yegorushka looked at him in surprise. At that instant there was a flash of lightning.

'It's all right, hit me,' repeated Dymov. And without waiting for Yegorushka to hit him or to speak to him, he jumped down and said: 'How dreary I am!'

Then, swaying from one leg to the other and moving his shoulder-blades, he sauntered lazily alongside the string of waggons, and repeated in a voice half weeping, half angry:

'How dreary I am! Oh Lord! Don't you take offence, Emelyan,' he said as he passed Emelyan. 'Ours is a wretched cruel life!'

There was a flash of lightning on the right, and, like a reflection in the looking-glass, at once a second flash in the distance.

'Yegory, take this,' cried Panteley, throwing up something big and dark.

'What is it?' asked Yegorushka.

'A mat. There will be rain, so cover yourself up.'

Yegorushka sat up and looked about him. The distance had grown perceptibly blacker, and now oftener than every minute winked with a pale light. The blackness was being bent towards the right as though by its own weight.

'Will there be a storm, Grandfather?' asked Yegorushka.

'Ah, my poor feet, how they ache!' Panteley said in a high-pitched voice, stamping his feet and not hearing the boy.

On the left someone seemed to strike a match in the sky; a pale phosphorescent streak gleamed and went out. There was a sound as though someone very far away were walking over an iron roof, probably barefoot, for the iron gave a hollow rumble.

'It's set in!' cried Kiruha.

Between the distance and the horizon on the right there was a flash of lightning so vivid that it lighted up part of the steppe and the spot where the clear sky met the blackness. A terrible cloud was swooping down, without haste, a compact mass; big black shreds pressing one upon another were piling up on the right and left horizon. The tattered, ragged look of the storm-cloud gave it a drunken disorderly air. There was a distinct, not smothered, growl of thunder. Yegorushka crossed himself and began quickly putting on his great-coat.

'I am dreary!' Dymov's shout floated from the foremost waggon, and it could be told from his voice that he was beginning to be ill-humoured again. 'I am so dreary!'

All at once there was a squall of wind, so violent that it almost snatched away Yegorushka's bundle and mat; the mat fluttered in all directions and flapped on the bale and on Yegorushka's face. The wind dashed whistling over the steppe, whirled round in disorder and raised such an uproar from the grass that neither the thunder nor the creaking of the wheels could be heard; it blew from the black storm-cloud, carrying with it clouds of dust and the scent of rain and wet earth. The moonlight grew mistier, as it were dirtier; the stars were even more overcast; and clouds of dust could be seen hurrying along the edge of the road, followed by their shadows. By now, most likely, the whirlwind eddying round and lifting from the earth dust, dry grass and feathers, was mounting to the very sky; uprooted plants must have been flying by that very black storm-cloud, and how frightened they must have been! But through the dust that clogged the eyes nothing could be seen but the flash of lightning.

Yegorushka, thinking it would pour with rain in a minute, knelt up and covered himself with the mat.

'Panteley-ey!' someone shouted in the front. 'A . . . a . . . va!'

'I can't!' Panteley answered in a loud high voice. 'A . . . a . . . va! Arya . . . a!'

There was an angry clap of thunder, which rolled across the sky from right to left, then back again, and died away near the foremost waggon.

'Holy, holy, holy, Lord of Saboath,' whispered Yegorushka, crossing himself. 'Fill Heaven and earth with Thy glory.'

The blackness in the sky yawned wide and breathed white fire. At once there was another clap of thunder. It had scarcely ceased when there was a flash of lightning so broad that Yegorushka suddenly saw through a slit in the mat the whole highroad to the very horizon, all the waggoners and even Kiruha's waistcoat. The black shreds had by now moved upwards from the left, and one of them, a coarse, clumsy monster like a claw with fingers, stretched to the moon.

Yegorushka made up his mind to shut his eyes tight, to pay no attention to it, and to wait till it was all over.

The rain was for some reason long in coming. Yegorushka peeped out from the mat in the hope that perhaps the storm-cloud was passing over. It was fearfully dark. Yegorushka could see neither Panteley, nor the bale of wool, nor himself; he looked sideways towards the place where the moon had lately been, but there was the same black darkness there as over the waggons. And in the darkness the flashes of lightning seemed more violent and blinding, so that they hurt his eyes.

'Panteley!' called Yegorushka.

No answer followed. But now a gust of wind for the last time flung up the mat and hurried away. A quiet regular sound was heard. A big cold drop fell on Yegorushka's knee, another trickled over his hand. He noticed that his knees were not covered, and tried to rearrange the mat, but at that moment something began pattering on the road, then on the shafts and the bales. It was the rain. As though they understood one another, the rain and the mat began prattling of something rapidly, gaily and most annoyingly like two magpies.

Yegorushka knelt up or rather squatted on his boots. While the rain was pattering on the mat, he leaned forward to screen his knees, which were suddenly wet. He succeeded in covering his knees, but in less than a minute was aware of a penetrating, unpleasant dampness behind on his back and the calves of his legs. He returned to his former position, exposing his knees to the rain, and wondered what to do to rearrange the mat, which he could not see in the darkness. But his arms were already wet, the water was trickling up his sleeves and down his collar, and his shoulder-blades felt chilly. And he made up his mind to do nothing but sit motionless and wait till it was all over.

'Holy, holy, holy!' he whispered.

Suddenly, exactly over his head, the sky cracked with a fearful deafening din; he huddled up and held his breath, waiting for the fragments to fall upon his head and back. He inadvertently opened his eyes and saw a blinding intense light flare out and flash five times on his fingers, his wet sleeves, and on the trickles of water running from the mat upon the bales and down to the ground. There was a fresh peal of thunder as violent and awful; the sky was not growling and rumbling now, but uttering short crashing sounds like the crackling of dry wood.

'Trrah! tah! tah! tah!' the thunder rang out distinctly, rolled over the sky, seemed to stumble, and somewhere by the foremost waggons or far behind to fall with an abrupt angry 'Trrra!'

The flashes of lightning had at first been only terrible, but with such thunder they seemed sinister and menacing. Their magic light pierced through closed eyelids and sent a chill all over the body. What could he do not to see them? Yegorushka made up his mind to turn over on his face. Cautiously, as though afraid of being watched, he got on all fours, and his hands slipping on the wet bale, he turned back again.

'Trrah! tah! tah!' floated over his head, rolled under the waggons and exploded 'Kraa!'

Again he inadvertently opened his eyes and saw a new danger: three huge giants with long pikes were following the waggon! A flash of lightning gleamed on the points of their pikes and lighted up their figures very distinctly. They were men of huge proportions, with covered faces, bowed heads, and heavy footsteps. They seemed gloomy and dispirited and lost in thought. Perhaps they were not following the waggons with any harmful intent, and yet there was something awful in their proximity.

Yegorushka turned quickly forward, and trembling all over, cried: 'Panteley! Grandfather!'

'Trrah! tah! tah!' the sky answered him.

He opened his eyes to see if the waggoners were there. There were flashes of lightning in two places, which lighted up the road to the far distance, the whole string of waggons and all the waggoners. Streams of water were flowing along the road and bubbles were dancing. Panteley was walking beside the waggon; his tall hat and his shoulder were covered with a small mat; his figure expressed neither terror nor uneasiness, as though he were deafened by the thunder and blinded by the lightning.

'Grandfather, the giants!' Yegorushka shouted to him in tears.

But the old man did not hear. Further away walked Emelyan. He was covered from head to foot with a big mat and was triangular in shape. Vassya, without anything over him, was walking with the same wooden step as usual, lifting his feet high and not bending his knees. In the flash of lightning it seemed as though the waggons were not moving and the men were motionless, that Vassya's lifted foot was rigid in the same position. . . .

Yegorushka called the old man once more. Getting no answer, he sat motionless, and no longer waited for it all to end. He was convinced that the thunder would kill him in another minute, and he would accidentally open his eyes and see the terrible giants, and he left off crossing himself, calling the old man and thinking of his mother, and was simply numb with cold and the conviction that the storm would never end.

But at last there was the sound of voices.

'Yegory, are you asleep?' Panteley cried below. 'Get down! Is he deaf, the silly little thing? . . .'

'Something like a storm!' said an unfamiliar bass voice, and the stranger cleared his throat as though he had just tossed off a good glass of vodka.

Yegorushka opened his eyes. Close to the waggon stood Panteley, Emelyan, looking like a triangle, and the giants. The latter were by now much shorter, and when Yegorushka looked more closely at them they turned out to be ordinary peasants, carrying on their shoulders not pikes but pitchforks. In the space between Panteley and the triangular figure, gleamed the window of a low-pitched hut. So the waggons were halting in the village. Yegorushka flung off the mat, took his bundle and made haste to get off the waggon. Now when close to him there were people talking and a lighted window he no longer felt afraid, though the thunder was crashing as before and the whole sky was streaked with lightning.

'It was a good storm, all right. . . .' Panteley was muttering. 'Thank God . . . my feet are a little softened by the rain. It was all right. . . . Have you got down, Yegory? Well, go into the hut; it is all right. . . .'

'Holy, holy, holy!' wheezed Emelyan, 'it must have struck something. . . . Are you of these parts?' he asked the giants.

'No, from Glinovo. We belong to Glinovo. We are working at the Platers'.'

'Threshing?'

'All sorts. Just now we are getting in the wheat. The light-ning, the lightning! It is long since we have had such a storm. . . .'

Yegorushka went into the hut. He was met by a lean hunchbacked old woman with a sharp chin. She stood holding a tallow candle in her hands, screwing up her eyes and heaving prolonged sighs.

'What a storm God has sent us!' she said. 'And our lads are out for the night on the steppe; they'll have had a bad time, poor dears! Take off your things, little sir, take off your things.'

Shivering with cold and shrugging squeamishly, Yegorushka pulled off his drenched overcoat, then stretched out his arms and straddled his legs, and stood a long time without moving. The slightest movement caused an unpleasant sensation of cold and wetness. His sleeves and the back of his shirt were sopped, his trousers stuck to his legs, his head was dripping.

'What's the use of standing there, with your legs apart, little lad?' said the old woman. 'Come, sit down.'

Holding his legs wide apart, Yegorushka went up to the table and sat down on a bench near somebody's head. The head moved, puffed a stream of air through its nose, made a chewing sound and subsided. A mound covered with a sheepskin stre-tched from the head along the bench; it was a peasant woman asleep.

The old woman went out sighing, and came back with a big water melon and a little sweet melon.

'Have something to eat, my dear! I have nothing else to offer you. . . .' she said, yawning. She rummaged in the table and took out a long sharp knife, very much like the one with which the brigands killed the merchants in the inn. 'Have some, my dear!'

Yegorushka, shivering as though he were in a fever, ate a slice of sweet melon with black bread and then a slice of water melon, and that made him feel colder still.

'Our lads are out on the steppe for the night. . . .' sighed the old woman while he was eating. 'The terror of the Lord! I'd light the candle under the ikon, but I don't know where Stepanida has put it. Have some more, little sir, have some more. . . .' The old woman gave a yawn and, putting her right hand behind her, scratched her left shoulder.

'It must be two o'clock now,' she said; 'it will soon be time to get up. Our lads are out on the steppe for the night; they are all wet through for sure. . . .'

'Granny,' said Yegorushka, 'I am sleepy.'

'Lie down, my dear, lie down,' the old woman sighed, yawning. 'Lord Jesus Christ! I was asleep, when I heard a noise as though someone were knocking. I woke up and looked, and it was the storm God had sent us. . . . I'd have lighted the candle, but I couldn't find it.'

Talking to herself, she pulled some rags, probably her own bed, off the bench, took two sheepskins off a nail by the stove, and began laying them out for a bed for Yegorushka. 'The storm doesn't grow less,' she muttered. 'If only nothing's struck in an unlucky hour. Our lads are out on the steppe for the night. Lie down and sleep, my dear. . . . Christ be with you, my child. . . . I won't take away the melon; maybe you'll have a bit when you get up.'

The sighs and yawns of the old woman, the even breathing of the sleeping woman, the half-darkness of the hut, and the sound of the rain outside, made one sleepy. Yegorushka was shy of undressing before the old woman. He only took off his boots, lay down and covered himself with the sheepskin.

'Is the little lad lying down?' he heard Panteley whisper a little later.

'Yes,' answered the old woman in a whisper. 'The terror of the Lord! It thunders and thunders, and there is no end to it.'

'It will soon be over,' wheezed Panteley, sitting down; 'it's quieter. . . . The lads have gone into the huts, and two have stayed with the horses. The lads have. . . . They can't; . . . the horses would be taken away. . . . I'll sit here for a bit and then go and take my turn. . . . We can't leave them; they would be taken. . . .'

Panteley and the old woman sat side by side at Yegorushka's feet, talking in hissing whispers and interspersing their speech with sighs and yawns. And Yegorushka could not get warm. The warm heavy sheepskin lay on him, but he was trembling all over; his arms and legs were twitching, and his whole inside was shivering. . . . He undressed under the sheepskin, but that was no good. His shivering grew more and more acute.

Panteley went out to take his turn with the horses, and afterwards came back again, and still Yegorushka was shivering all over and could not get to sleep. Something weighed upon his head and chest and oppressed him, and he did not know what it was, whether it was the old people whispering, or the heavy smell of the sheepskin. The melon he had eaten had left an unpleasant taste in his mouth. Moreover he was being bitten by fleas.

'Grandfather, I am cold,' he said, and did not know his own voice.

'Go to sleep, my child, go to sleep,' sighed the old woman.

Tit came up to the bedside on his thin little legs and waved his arms, then grew up to the ceiling and turned into a windmill. . . . Father Christopher, not as he was in the chaise, but in his full vestments with the sprinkler in his hand, walked round the mill, sprinkling it with holy water, and it left off waving. Yegorushka, knowing this was delirium, opened his eyes.

'Grandfather,' he called, 'give me some water.'

No one answered. Yegorushka felt it insufferably stifling and uncomfortable lying down. He got up, dressed, and went out of the hut. Morning was beginning. The sky was overcast, but it was no longer raining. Shivering and wrapping himself in his wet overcoat, Yegorushka walked about the muddy yard and listened to the silence; he caught sight of a little shed with a half-open door made of reeds. He looked into this shed, went into it, and sat down in a dark corner on a heap of dry dung.

There was a tangle of thoughts in his heavy head; his mouth was dry and unpleasant from the metallic taste. He looked at his hat, straightened the peacock's feather on it, and thought how he had gone with his mother to buy the hat. He put his hand into his pocket and took out a lump of brownish sticky paste. How had that paste come into his pocket? He thought a minute, smelt it; it smelt of honey. Aha! it was the Jewish cake! How sopped it was, poor thing!

Yegorushka examined his coat. It was a little grey overcoat

with big bone buttons, cut in the shape of a frock-coat. At home, being a new and expensive article, it had not been hung in the hall, but with his mother's dresses in her bedroom; he was only allowed to wear it on holidays. Looking at it, Yegorushka felt sorry for it. He thought that he and the great-coat were both abandoned to the mercy of destiny; he thought that he would never get back home, and began sobbing so violently that he almost fell off the heap of dung.

A big white dog with woolly tufts like curl-papers about its face, sopping from the rain, came into the shed and stared with curiosity at Yegorushka. It seemed to be hesitating whether to bark or not. Deciding that there was no need to bark, it went cautiously up to Yegorushka, ate the sticky plaster and went out again.

'There are Varlamov's men!' someone shouted in the street.

After having his cry out, Yegorushka went out of the shed and, walking round a big puddle, made his way towards the street. The waggons were standing exactly opposite the gateway. The drenched waggoners, with their muddy feet, were sauntering beside them or sitting on the shafts, as listless and drowsy as flies in autumn. Yegorushka looked at them and thought: 'How dreary and comfortless to be a peasant!' He went up to Panteley and sat down beside him on the shaft.

'Grandfather, I'm cold,' he said, shivering and thrusting his hands up his sleeves.

'Never mind, we shall soon be there,' yawned Panteley. 'Never mind, you will get warm.'

It must have been early when the waggons set off, for it was not hot. Yegorushka lay on the bales of wool and shivered with cold, though the sun soon came out and dried his clothes, the bales, and the earth. As soon as he closed his eyes he saw Tit and the windmill again. Feeling a sickness and heaviness all over, he did his utmost to drive away these images, but as soon as they vanished the daredevil Dymov, with red eyes and lifted fists, rushed at Yegorushka with a roar, or there was the sound of his complaint: 'I am so dreary!' Varlamov rode by on his little Cossack stallion; happy Konstantin passed, with a smile and the bustard in his arms. And how tedious these people were, how sickening and unbearable!

Once – it was towards evening – he raised his head to ask for water. The waggons were standing on a big bridge across a broad river. There was black smoke below over the river, and through it could be seen a steamer with a barge in tow. Ahead of them, beyond the river, was a huge mountain dotted with houses and churches; at the foot of the mountain an engine was being shunted along beside some goods trucks. . . .

Yegorushka had never before seen steamers, nor engines, nor broad rivers. Glancing at them now, he was not alarmed or surprised; there was not even a look of anything like curiosity in his face. He merely felt sick, and made haste to turn over to the edge of the bale. He was sick. Panteley, seeing this, cleared his throat and shook his head.

'Our little lad's taken ill,' he said. 'He must have got a chill to the stomach. The little lad must . . . away from home; it's a bad look-out!'

CHAPTER VIII

The waggons stopped at a big inn for merchants, not far from the quay. As Yegorushka climbed down from the waggon he heard a very familiar voice. Someone was helping him to get down, and saying:

'We arrived yesterday evening. . . . We have been expecting you all day. We meant to overtake you yesterday, but it was out of our way; we came by the other road. I say, how you have crumpled your coat! You'll catch it from your uncle!'

Yegorushka looked into the speaker's mottled face and remembered that this was Deniska.

'Your uncle and Father Christopher are in the inn now, drinking tea; come along!'

And he led Yegorushka to a big two-storied building, dark and gloomy like the almshouse at N. After going across the entry, up a dark staircase and through a narrow corridor, Yegorushka and Deniska reached a little room in which Ivan Ivanitch and Father Christopher were sitting at the tea-table. Seeing the boy, both the old men showed surprise and pleasure.

'Aha! Yegor Ni-ko-la-aitch!' chanted Father Christopher. 'Mr Lomonosov!'

'Ah, our gentleman that is to be,' said Kuzmitchov, 'pleased to see you!'

Yegorushka took off his great-coat, kissed his uncle's hand and Father Christopher's, and sat down to the table.

'Well, how did you like the journey, *puer bone?*' Father Christopher pelted him with questions as he poured him out some tea, with his radiant smile. 'Sick of it, I've no doubt? God save us all from having to travel by waggon or with oxen. You go on and on, God forgive us; you look ahead and the steppe is always lying stretched out the same as it was – you can't see the end of it! It's not travelling but regular torture. Why don't you drink your tea? Drink it up; and in your absence, while you have been trailing along with the waggons, we have settled all our business capitally. Thank God we have sold our wool to Tcherepahin, and no one could wish to have done better. . . . We have made a good bargain.'

At the first sight of his own people Yegorushka felt an overwhelming desire to complain. He did not listen to Father Christopher, but thought how to begin and what exactly to complain of. But Father Christopher's voice, which seemed to him harsh and unpleasant, prevented him from concentrating his attention and confused his thoughts. He had not sat at the table five minutes before he got up, went to the sofa and lay down.

'Well, well,' said Father Christopher in surprise. 'What about your tea?'

Still thinking what to complain of, Yegorushka leaned his head against the wall and broke into sobs.

'Well, well!' repeated Father Christopher, getting up and going to the sofa. 'Yegory, what is the matter with you? Why are you crying?'

'I'm . . . I'm ill,' Yegorushka brought out.

'Ill?' said Father Christopher in amazement. 'That's not the right thing, my boy. . . . One mustn't be ill on a journey. Aie, aie, what are you thinking about, boy . . . eh?'

He put his hand to Yegorushka's head, touched his cheek and said:

'Yes, your head's feverish. . . . You must have caught cold or else have eaten something. . . . Pray to God.'

'Should we give him quinine? . . .' said Ivan Ivanitch, troubled.

'No; he ought to have something hot. . . . Yegory, have a little drop of soup? Eh?'

'I . . . don't want any,' said Yegorushka.

'Are you feeling chilly?'

'I was chilly before, but now . . . now I am hot. And I ache all over. . . .'

Ivan Ivanitch went up to the sofa, touched Yegorushka on the head, cleared his throat with a perplexed air, and went back to the table.

'I tell you what, you undress and go to bed,' said Father Christopher. 'What you want is sleep now.'

He helped Yegorushka to undress, gave him a pillow and covered him with a quilt, and over that Ivan Ivanitch's great-coat. Then he walked away on tiptoe and sat down to the table. Yegorushka shut his eyes, and at once it seemed to him that he was not in the hotel room, but on the highroad beside the camp fire. Emelyan waved his hands, and Dymov with red eyes lay on his stomach and looked mockingly at Yegorushka.

'Beat him, beat him!' shouted Yegorushka.

'He is delirious,' said Father Christopher in an undertone.

'It's a nuisance!' sighed Ivan Ivanitch.

'He must be rubbed with oil and vinegar. Please God, he will be better tomorrow.'

To be rid of bad dreams, Yegorushka opened his eyes and began looking towards the fire. Father Christopher and Ivan Ivanitch had now finished their tea and were talking in a whisper. The first was smiling with delight, and evidently could not forget that he had made a good bargain over his wool; what delighted him was not so much the actual profit he had made, as the thought that on getting home he would gather round him his big family, wink slyly and go off into a chuckle; at first he would deceive them all, and say that he had sold the wool at a price below its value, then he would give his son-in-law, Mihail, a fat pocket-book and say: 'Well, take it! that's the way to do business!' Kuzmitchov did not seem pleased; his face expressed, as before, a business-like reserve and anxiety.

'If I could have known that Tcherepahin would give such a price,' he said in a low voice, 'I wouldn't have sold Makarov those five tons at home. It is vexatious! But who could have told that the price had gone up here?'

A man in a white shirt cleared away the samovar and lighted the little lamp before the ikon in the corner. Father Christopher whispered something in his ear; the man looked, made a serious face like a conspirator, as though to say, 'I understand,' went out, and returned a little while afterwards and put something under the sofa. Ivan Ivanitch made himself a bed on the floor, yawned several times, said his prayers lazily, and lay down.

'I think of going to the cathedral tomorrow,' said Father Christopher. 'I know the sacristan there. I ought to go and see the bishop after mass, but they say he is ill.'

He yawned and put out the lamp. Now there was no light in the room but the little lamp before the ikon.

'They say he can't receive visitors,' Father Christopher went on, undressing. 'So I shall go away without seeing him.'

He took off his full coat, and Yegorushka saw Robinson Crusoe reappear. Robinson stirred something in a saucer, went up to Yegorushka and whispered:

'Lomonosov, are you asleep? Sit up; I'm going to rub you with oil and vinegar. It's a good thing, only you must say a prayer.'

Yegorushka roused himself quickly and sat up. Father Christopher pulled down the boy's shirt, and shrinking and breathing jerkily, as though he were being tickled himself, began rubbing Yegorushka's chest.

'In the name of the Father, the Son, and the Holy Ghost,' he whispered, 'lie with your back upwards – that's it. . . . You'll be all right tomorrow, but don't do it again. . . . You are as hot as fire. I suppose you were on the road in the storm.'

'Yes.'

'You might well fall ill! In the name of the Father, the Son, and the Holy Ghost. . . . you might well fall ill!'

After rubbing Yegorushka, Father Christopher put on his shirt again, covered him, made the sign of the cross over him, and walked away. Then Yegorushka saw him saying his prayers. Probably the old man knew a great many prayers by heart, for he stood a long time before the ikon murmuring. After saying his prayers he made the sign of the cross over the window, the door, Yegorushka, and Ivan Ivanitch, lay down on the little sofa without a pillow, and covered himself with his full coat. A clock in the corridor struck ten. Yegorushka thought how long a time it would be before morning; feeling miserable, he pressed his forehead against the back of the sofa and left off trying to get rid of the oppressive misty dreams. But morning came much sooner than he expected.

It seemed to him that he had not been lying long with his head pressed to the back of the sofa, but when he opened his eyes slanting rays of sunlight were already shining on the floor

through the two windows of the little hotel room. Father
Christopher and Ivan Ivanitch were not in the room. The
room had been tidied; it was bright, snug, and smelt of Father
Christopher, who always smelt of cypress and dried cornflowers (at home he used to make the holy-water sprinklers
and decorations for the ikon stands out of cornflowers, and so
he was saturated with the smell of them). Yegorushka looked
at the pillow, at the slanting sunbeams, at his boots, which had
been cleaned and were standing side by side near the sofa, and
laughed. It seemed strange to him that he was not on the bales
of wool, that everything was dry around him, and that there
was no thunder and lightning on the ceiling.

He jumped off the sofa and began dressing. He felt splendid;
nothing was left of his yesterday's illness but a slight weakness
in his legs and neck. So the vinegar and oil had done good. He
remembered the steamer, the railway engine, and the broad
river, which he had dimly seen the day before, and now he
made haste to dress, to run to the quay and have a look at
them. When he had washed and was putting on his red shirt,
the latch of the door clicked, and Father Christopher appeared
in the doorway, wearing his top-hat and a brown silk cassock
over his canvas coat and carrying his staff in his hand. Smiling
and radiant (old men are always radiant when they come back
from church), he put a roll of holy bread and a parcel of some
sort on the table, prayed before the ikon, and said:

'God has sent us blessings – well, how are you?'

'Quite well now,' answered Yegorushka, kissing his hand.

'Thank God. . . . I have come from mass. . . . I've been to
see a sacristan I know. He invited me to breakfast with him,
but I didn't go. I don't like visiting people too early, God bless
them!'

He took off his cassock, stroked himself on the chest, and
without haste undid the parcel. Yegorushka saw a little tin of
caviare, a piece of dry-sturgeon, and a French loaf.

'See; I passed a fish-shop and brought this,' said Father
Christopher. 'There is no need to indulge in luxuries on an
ordinary weekday; but I thought, I've an invalid at home, so it
is excusable. And the caviare is good, real sturgeon. . . .'

The man in the white shirt brought in the samovar and a
tray with tea-things.

'Eat some,' said Father Christopher, spreading the caviare on a slice of bread and handing it to Yegorushka. 'Eat now and enjoy yourself, but the time will soon come for you to be studying. Mind you study with attention and application, so that good may come of it. What you have to learn by heart, learn by heart, but when you have to tell the inner sense in your own words, without regard to the outer form, then say it in your own words. And try to master all subjects. One man knows mathematics excellently, but has never heard of Pyotr Mogila; another knows about Pyotr Mogila, but cannot explain about the moon. But you study so as to understand everything. Study Latin, French, German. . . . geography, of course, history, theology, philosophy, mathematics, . . . and when you have mastered everything, not with haste but with prayer and with zeal, then go into the service. When you know everything it will be easy for you in any line of life. . . . You study and strive for the divine blessing, and God will show you what to be. Whether a doctor, a judge or an engineer. . . .'

Father Christopher spread a little caviare on a piece of bread, put it in his mouth and said:

'The Apostle Paul says: "Do not apply yourself to strange and diverse studies". Of course, if it is black magic, unlawful arts, or calling up spirits from the other world, like Saul, or studying subjects that can be of no use to yourself or others, better not learn them. You must undertake only what God has blessed. Take example . . . the Holy Apostles spoke in all languages, so you study languages. Basil the Great studied mathematics and philosophy – so you study them; St. Nestor wrote history – so you study and write history. Take example from the saints.'

Father Christopher sipped the tea from his saucer, wiped his moustaches, and shook his head.

'Good!' he said. 'I was educated in the old-fashioned way; I have forgotten a great deal by now, but still I live differently from other people. Indeed, there is no comparison. For instance, in company at a dinner, or at an assembly, one says something in Latin, or makes some allusion from history or philosophy, and it pleases people, and it pleases me myself. . . . Or when the circuit court comes and one has to

take the oath, all the other priests are shy, but I am quite at home
with the judges, the prosecutors, and the lawyers. I talk intel-
lectually, drink a cup of tea with them, laugh, ask them what I
don't know. . . . and they like it. So that's how it is, my boy.
Learning is light and ignorance is darkness. Study! It's hard, of
course; nowadays study is expensive. . . . Your mother is a
widow; she lives on her pension, but there, of course. . . .'

Father Christopher glanced apprehensively towards the
door, and went on in a whisper:

'Ivan Ivanitch will assist. He won't desert you. He has no
children of his own, and he will help you. Don't be uneasy.'

He looked grave, and whispered still more softly:

'Only mind, Yegory, don't forget your mother and Ivan
Ivanitch, God preserve you from it. The commandment bids
you honour your mother, and Ivan Ivanitch is your benefactor
and takes the place of a father to you. If you become learned,
God forbid you should be impatient and scornful with people
because they are not so clever as you, then woe, woe to you!'

Father Christopher raised his hand and repeated in a thin
voice:

'Woe to you! Woe to you!'

Father Christopher's tongue was loosened, and he was, as
they say, warming to his subject; he would not have finished till
dinnertime but the door opened and Ivan Ivanitch walked in.
He said good-morning hurriedly, sat down to the table, and
began rapidly swallowing his tea.

'Well, I have settled all our business,' he said. 'We might have
gone home today, but we have still to think about Yegor. We
must arrange for him. My sister told me that Nastasya Petrovna, a friend of hers, lives somewhere here, so perhaps she
will take him in as a boarder.'

He rummaged in his pocket-book, found a crumpled note
and read:

'"Little Lower Street: Nastasya Petrovna Toskunov, living
in a house of her own," We must go at once and try to find her.
It's a nuisance!'

Soon after breakfast Ivan Ivanitch and Yegorushka left the
inn.

'It's a nuisance!' muttered his uncle. 'You are sticking to me
like a burr. You and your mother want education and gen-

tlemanly breeding and I have nothing but worry with you both. . . .'

When they crossed the yard, the waggons and the drivers were not there. They had all gone off to the quay early in the morning. In a far-off dark corner of the yard stood the chaise.

'Good-bye, chaise!' thought Yegorushka.

At first they had to go a long way uphill by a broad street, then they had to cross a big market-place; here Ivan Ivanitch asked a policeman for Little Lower Street.

'I say,' said the policeman, with a grin, 'it's a long way off, out that way towards the town grazing ground.'

They met several cabs but Ivan Ivanitch only permitted himself such a weakness as taking a cab in exceptional cases and on great holidays. Yegorushka and he walked for a long while through paved streets, then along streets where there were only wooden planks at the sides and no pavements, and in the end got to streets where there were neither planks nor pavements. When their legs and their tongues had brought them to Little Lower Street they were both red in the face, and taking off their hats, wiped away the perspiration.

'Tell me, please,' said Ivan Ivanitch, addressing an old man sitting on a little bench by a gate, 'where is Nastasya Petrovna Toskunov's house?'

'There is no one called Toskunov here,' said the old man, after pondering a moment. 'Perhaps it's Timoshenko you want.'

'No, Toskunov. . . .'

'Excuse me, there's no one called Toskunov. . . .'

Ivan Ivanitch shrugged his shoulders and trudged on farther.

'You needn't look,' the old man called after them. 'I tell you there isn't, and there isn't.'

'Listen, auntie,' said Ivan Ivanitch, addressing an old woman who was siting at a corner with a tray of pears and sunflower seeds, 'where is Nastasya Petrovna Toskunov's house?'

The old woman looked at him with surprise and laughed.

'Why, Nastasya Petrovna live in her own house now!' she cried. 'Lord! it is eight years since she married her daughter and gave up the house to her son-in-law! It's her son-in-law lives there now.'

And her eyes expressed: 'How is it you didn't know a simple thing like that, you fools?'

'And where does she live now?' Ivan Ivanitch asked.

'Oh, Lord!' cried the old woman, flinging up her hands in surprise. 'She moved ever so long ago! It's eight years since she gave up her house to her son-in-law! Upon my word!'

She probably expected Ivan Ivanitch to be surprised, too, and to exclaim: 'You don't say so,' but Ivan Ivanitch asked very calmly:

'Where does she live now?'

The old woman tucked up her sleeves and, stretching out her bare arm to point, shouted in a shrill piercing voice:

'Go straight on, straight on, straight on. You will pass a little red house, then you will see a little alley on your left. Turn down that little alley, and it will be the third gate on the right. . . .'

Ivan Ivanitch and Yegorushka reached the little red house, turned to the left down the little alley, and made for the third gate on the right. On both sides of this very old grey gate there was a grey fence with big gaps in it. The first part of the fence was tilting forwards and threatened to fall, while on the left of the gate it sloped backwards towards the yard. The gate itself stood upright and seemed to be still undecided which would suit it best – to fall forwards or backwards. Ivan Ivanitch opened the little gate at the side, and he and Yegorushka saw a big yard overgrown with weeds and burdocks. A hundred paces from the gate stood a little house with a red roof and green shutters. A stout woman with her sleeves tucked up and her apron held out was standing in the middle of the yard, scattering something on the ground and shouting in a voice as shrill as that of the woman selling fruit:

'Chick! . . . Chick! . . . Chick!'

Behind her sat a red dog with pointed ears. Seeing the strangers, he ran to the little gate and broke into a tenor bark (all red dogs have a tenor bark).

'Whom do you want?' asked the woman, putting up her hand to shade her eyes from the sun.

'Good-morning!' Ivan Ivanitch shouted, too, waving off the red dog with his stick. 'Tell me, please, does Nastasya Petrovna Toskunov live here?'

'Yes! But what do you want with her?'

'Perhaps you are Nastasya Petrovna?'

'Well, yes, I am!'

'Very pleased to see you. . . . You see, your old friend Olga Ivanovna Knyasev sends her love to you. This is her little son. And I, perhaps you remember, am her brother Ivan Ivanitch. . . . You are one of us from N. . . . You were born among us and married there. . . .'

A silence followed. The stout woman stared blankly at Ivan Ivanitch, as though not believing or not understanding him, then she flushed all over, and flung up her hands; the oats were scattered out of her apron and tears spurted from her eyes.

'Olga Ivanovna!' she screamed, breathless with excitement. 'My own darling! Ah, holy saints, why am I standing here like a fool? My pretty little angel. . . .'

She embraced Yegorushka, wetted his face with her tears, and broke down completely.

'Heavens!' she said, wringing her hands, 'Olga's little boy! How delightful! He is his mother all over! The image of his mother! But why are you standing in the yard? Come indoors.'

Crying, gasping for breath and talking as she went, she hurried towards the house. Her visitors trudged after her.

'The room has not been done yet,' she said, ushering the visitors into a stuffy little drawing-room adorned with many ikons and pots of flowers. 'Oh, Mother of God! Vassilisa, go and open the shutters anyway! My little angel! My little beauty! I did not know that Olitchka had a boy like that!'

When she had calmed down and got over her first surprise Ivan Ivanitch asked to speak to her alone. Yegorushka went into another room; there was a sewing-machine; in the window was a cage with a starling in it, and there were as many ikons and flowers as in the drawing-room. Near the machine stood a little girl with a sunburnt face and chubby cheeks like Tit's, and a clean cotton dress. She stared at Yegorushka without blinking, and apparently felt very awkward. Yegorushka looked at her and after a pause asked:

'What's your name?'

The little girl moved her lips, looked as if she were going to cry, and answered softly:

'Atka. . . .'

This meant Katka.

'He will live with you,' Ivan Ivanitch was whispering in the drawing-room, 'if you will be so kind, and we will pay ten roubles a month for his keep. He is not a spoilt boy; he is quiet. . . .'

'I really don't know what to say, Ivan Ivanitch!' Nastasya Petrovna sighed tearfully. 'Ten roubles a month is very good, but it is a dreadful thing to take another person's child! He may fall ill or something. . . .'

When Yegorushka was summoned back to the drawing-room Ivan Ivanitch was standing with his hat in his hands, saying good-bye.

'Well, let him stay with you now, then.' he said. 'Good-bye! You stay, Yegor!' he said, addressing his nephew. 'Don't be troublesome; mind you obey Nastasya Petrovna. . . . Good-bye; I am coming again tomorrow.'

And he went away. Nastasya once more embraced Yegorushka, called him a little angel, and with a tear-stained face began preparing for dinner. Three minutes later Yegorushka was sitting beside her, answering her endless questions and eating hot savoury cabbage soup.

In the evening he sat again at the same table and, resting his head on his hand, listened to Nastasya Petrovna. Alternately laughing and crying, she talked of his mother's young days, her own marriage, her children. . . . A cricket chirruped in the stove, and there was a faint humming from the burner of the lamp. Nastasya Petrovna talked in a low voice, and was continually dropping her thimble in her excitement; and Katya her granddaughter, crawled under the table after it and each time sat a long while under the table, probably examining Yegorushka's feet; and Yegorushka listened, half dozing and looking at the old woman's face, her wart with hairs on it, and the stains of tears, . . . and he felt sad, very sad. He was put to sleep on a chest and told that if he were hungry in the night he must go out into the little passage and take some chicken, put there under a plate in the window.

Next morning Ivan Ivanitch and Father Christopher came to say goodbye. Nastasya Petrovna was delighted to see them, and was about to set the samovar; but Ivan Ivanitch, who was in a great hurry, waved his hands and said:

'We have no time for tea! We are just setting off.'

Before parting they all sat down and were silent for a minute. Nastasya Petrovna heaved a deep sigh and looked towards the ikon with tear-stained eyes.

'Well,' began Ivan Ivanitch, getting up, 'so you will stay. . . .'

All at once the look of business-like reserve vanished from his face; he flushed a little and said with a mournful smile:

'Mind you work hard. . . . Don't forget your mother, and obey Nastasya Petrovna. . . . If you are diligent at school, Yegor, I'll stand by you.'

He took his purse out of his pocket, turned his back to Yegorushka, fumbled for a long time among the smaller coins, and, finding a ten-kopeck piece, gave it to Yegorushka.

Father Christopher, without haste, blessed Yegorushka.

'In the name of the Father, the Son, and the Holy Ghost. . . . Study,' he said. 'Work hard, my lad. If I die, remember me in your prayers. Here is a ten-kopeck piece from me, too. . . .'

Yegorushka kissed his hand, and shed tears; something whispered in his heart that he would never see the old man again.

'I have applied at the high school already,' said Ivan Ivanitch in a voice as though there were a corpse in the room. 'You will take him for the entrance examination on the seventh of August. . . . Well, good-bye; God bless you, good-bye. Yegor!'

'You might at least have had a cup of tea,' wailed Nastasya Petrovna.

Through the tears that filled his eyes Yegorushka could not see his uncle and Father Christopher go out. He rushed to the window, but they were not in the yard, and the red dog, who had just been barking, was running back from the gate with the air of having done his duty. Yegorushka, he could not have said why, leapt up and flew out of the room. When he ran out of the gate Ivan Ivanitch and Father Christopher, the former waving his stick with the crook, the latter his staff, were just turning the corner. Yegorushka felt that with these people all that he had known till then had vanished from him for ever. He sank helplessly on to the little bench, and with bitter tears greeted the new unknown life that was beginning for him now. . . .

What would that life be like?